The Wander Daze
Part 1

and

Things Go Wrong:
The Wander Daze
Part 2

Richard Lapinski, Jr

THE WANDER DAZE PART 1 AND THINGS GO WRONG: THE WANDER DAZE PART 2

iUniverse books may be ordered through booksellers or by contacting:

iUniverse
1663 Liberty Drive
Bloomington, IN 47403
www.iuniverse.com
844-349-9409

ISBN: 978-1-6632-4154-2 (sc)
ISBN: 978-1-6632-4153-5 (e)

Print information available on the last page.

iUniverse rev. date: 07/05/2022

DEDICATION

This book is dedicated to my wife Tammi, where sometimes living with me is not as humorous being a coworker of friend. Lauren for being a fantastic daughter. And, last but not least my son Alex for coming up with the title of this book.

CONTENTS

PART 2

THE WANDER DAZE
Part 1

CHAPTER 1

Slip Sliding Away

There is nothing but total darkness. All you hear is a buzzing background noise.

ZZZZZZZZ.

Slowly the darkness fades and you see a man in ripped blue jeans, an old 1977 Farrah Fawcett T-shirt and an open wind breaker with I AM NOT A SN ITCH lettered on the back.

Next the scene shifts to a stream of 100 unsuspecting seniors in single file line shuffling along. Walkers are clacking, wheel chairs are hissing and footsteps are pounding. All of a sudden, a frail-looking 90-something senior unexpectedly slips on the frictionless waxed floor. All you see is the look of despair in the face of the falling senior. She falls into an 85-year-old man with a pot belly and a five o'clock shadow. He loses control of his cane and goes tumbling as well. By now you get the picture, one dead beat old geezer after another falling on top of each other. Captured on film or even the naked eye, it looks like human dominoes falling one after another, until before you know it the corridor is flooded with old bodies scattered across the floor, as far as the eye can see. Incomprehensible words, screams, crying fill the air, it is mass hysteria. Quickly CNA

Janey runs out with her stethoscope and blood pressure cuff, frazzled beyond belief.

I need to hurry up and get vital signs on all I 00 of these old farts. Whichone should I do first?

Fellow CNA Rachel watches Janey with a look of both bemusement and disgust.

What in the world is wrong with you, Janey, you would never make it on the night shift with that hurry-up attitude and manner of yours.

What do you mean?

You've got to pace yourself, Janey, getting yourself worked up into a frenzy and racing around here looking for stethoscopes, like a chicken with his head cut off, you are going to bum yourself out.

What do you mean?

I mean you have to slow down and not panic. First thing you do when you see all those deadbeats hit the ground is head for the break room and get a soda and a snack. That is presuming you are not in the middle of a good movie or an interesting book.

Why would I do that?

AHHH, I can see this is going to be harder than I thought, you are so naive, Janey! Because if you are not around and no one sees you, you don't have to clean up this mess.

But what about the residents, they are on the ground, they might be hurt? Janey, they have already fallen, there is nowhere else for them to go. If they are hurt, you racing over there to do vital signs isn't going to make them any better. Besides, the quicker you get them up, the quicker they are just going to fall again. It is too late now because we are already over here, and everyone is looking at us, so I will help you out this time, but don't let this happen again or you are on your own.

How would you like to be lying on that stinky floor? Janey, old people like to stink!

What, oh that is awful, how could you be so mean and cruel?

I've been a CNA for IO years, Janey, how long have you been a CNA, like 3 months? I am telling you, old people like to stink. If I had a nickel for every time I tried to clean up a resident or give one a shower, thinking I would make them feel better, and they yelled rape, murder, leave me alone, you asshole etc., and they...started hitting and biting me, I would be a billionaire.

Why would they do that?

Because they like to stink and don't want to be bathed! Well, maybe you are right.

Of course, I am right.

Wouldn't you know it, just like Murphy's law states: if something can go wrong it will, and you can't get any more wrong than Nurse Dee Dee. As she is popping diet pills and eating a funnel cake Nurse Dee Dee overhears the CNAs conversation and waddles over to chastise them.

Such language is abuse and will not be tolerated. I am sorry, ma' am, it will never happen again.

Me too, agrees Rachel.

Well, OK, in addition to being an excellent Nurse, I have accepted Jesus Christ as my Lord and Savior, so I will forgive you.

Thank you, Nurse Dee Dee. Thank you, Nurse Dee Dee.

You are welcome, now take care and comfort my residents.

Yes, ma'am.

Yes, ma'am.

Still, Rachel can't help but wonder if that hypocritical scumbag Nurse Dee Dee is not going to rat them out and blab to President Dewey Screwem and Vice President Ann Howe.

While all of this is going on, Nurse Tilly is behind the desk frantically shuffling through incident report forms, trying in vain to get 100 copies. Looks like Buster, in customer service, needs to get off his fat ass and go and make some copies.

Meanwhile, back on the floor, you hear moans of:

Tiff, Tiff, Hail Mary full of grace the Lord is with you. My legs are aching like anything.

Nurse, Nurse, I'm on the floor, help me now, Nurse.

Oh don't, I don't like it that way.

Oh Lordy, Lordy, I be hurting' so bad it's like I done died five times over. I need help, I need help.

One man, who looks fairly well preserved physically for an old timer, asks if he could get up, and get some food for a horse?

With only two stand up lifts and one hoyer lift in the whole complex, it could be days before all these dead beats are up off the ground.

Good thing there is a bright young kid working in laundry, who is considerate enough to take time away from watching TV, to occasionally throw some garments in the washing machine. At least, there will be clean blankets for the residents to bundle up with while they camp out on the floor overnight.

CHAPTER 2
Pseudo-Studies

This is where I have a bone to pick with the so-called experts, who sit around all day and dream up ways to prevent seniors from falling. How do they know seniors don't like to fall? What else do they have to do besides sleep, go to the bathroom, and ingest tons of pain killers? After all, do we really do anything that we don't like to? I am telling you, seniors like to fall! I mean why do you eat out at restaurants, why do you join a bowling league, why do you watch TV or eat strawberry ice cream? Because you like to. None of us do anything we don't like to. Sure, you can argue that addicts engage in activities every day that they don't like, but I ask you, has anyone ever seen a study from John Hopkins University or Harvard Medical School that says falling is an addiction? I think not. I would argue also that, initially, addicts do get a great deal of satisfaction out of their vice, it just got out of hand.

It is totally unnecessary to devise programs like "Fall Prevention, Breaking the Cycle." What cycle?

Even if someone could convince me that the elderly do not like to fall, falls are at an all-time low. No program has to be put in place for a student who averages 98% on all his or her tests.

Look at these figures, aren't they astounding, isn't it incredible how skilled the CNAs and Nurses are? At FeudalCare Nursing Home there are about 100 residents. It is possible that a resident could fall every hour. There are 24 hours in a day. 7 days a week. Approximately 30 days in a month and 365 days a year. So:

> 100 residents
> 24 hours a day
> 2400 possible falls a day
> 365 days a year
> 876,000 possible falls a year
> 156 actual falls a year
> 875,844 falls prevented

Suddenly, even though it is 2005, the song "We're Gonna Party Like it is 1999" blares over the PA system. Gradually the music softens until there is total silence. FeudalCare President Dewey Screwem grabs the microphone. Ladies and Gentlemen, welcome to the Louisiana Super Dome for tonight's EXTRAVAGANZA!! CAN YOU BELIEVE IT? I want to congratulate all the dedicated CNAs and Nurses for preventing approximately 876,000 falls and potential broken bones this year. In order for us to show our undying (pun intended) appreciation for a job well done, we have spared no expense. Just like one of Jennifer Lopez's weddings.

Upon completion of Screwem's diatribe, dehydrated Aides and Nurses stampede over to the open bar, like soldiers storming the beach at Normandy. Then it is on to the appetizer table to satisfy their famished gullets on boiled shrimp and caviar. Forty-five minutes later a bell sounds, which could mean only one thing: dinner is served. Angus prime rib followed by bananas foster for dessert. Dinner and dessert is immediately followed by live entertainment from one of the world's premiere bands. The entertainers take a break and once again President Screwem takes the microphone.

Ladies and Gentlemen, let us bow our heads in a moment of silence to thank the Big Fella upstairs forth is delicious feast and for blessing us with the opportunity to be employed by FeudalCare. I want to personally thank him for such a fine work force. Oh, and by the way, thanks also for a record money-making year.

Speeches, awards, presentations, and high fives honor these magnificent heroes for their success in fall and broken bone prevention. Tearful family members take the podium, thanking FeudalCare CNAs and Nurses for the tens of thousands of falls and broken bones spared their loved ones.

Protecting and preventing residents from falling is all that matters, a beaming Screwem shouts into the microphone. It's all about insuring our loved ones' safety, a somber Vice President Ann Howe chimes in. All of the FeudalCare Associates had an absolutely marvelous time at the party. V.P. Howe took it upon herself to make sure all her prized employees got back to their penthouse suites at the Hilton Hotel safely by personally chauffeuring the limousine. Ann is a fine Christian woman who abstains from all alcoholic beverages (you know, treat your body like a temple) so she was the only one in any condition to drive. Of course Ann would never begrudge her Aides and Nurses of tipping back a few cocktails (judge not, least you be judged). Ann is very uncomfortable forcing her views on other people.

The following day all CNAs and Nurses were jetted back home in the company's private Lear Jet. Needless to say, all involved had an absolutely wonderful and unforgettable experience.

The dreaming FeudalCare CNA wakes up and is quickly brought back to reality with a thud, like a 2 by 4 hitting him smack across the face. President Screwem and V. P. Howe are FURIOUS! And they severely reprimand the CNA for dozing off How dare a lowly Aide fall asleep at such an important meeting discussing fall prevention.

At all costs, FeudalCare Management must break something that is fixed. Moronic ideas such as hipsters and body alarms are now going to be installed at break neck speed (pun intended). Hipsters really are a stroke of genius! At least it was for the con man who duped the entire Elder Industry. He somehow miraculously convinced Old People Executives into believing that 2 flimsy egg cartons sewed into a pair of underwear are going to protect bones. Bones so brittle that if it was not for the burlap sack referred to as skin, you could pick them up and blow the dust into the atmosphere. Hipsters are based on the same philosophy, that if you stack a few mattresses together you can jump off the hundredth floor of the Empire State Building without so much as a scratch.

Selective objectivity and selective amnesia are very important to any huge corporation and FeudalCare is no exception. Smoke and mirrors, symbolism over substance, whatever you want to call it, FeudalCare is a master. You see, it really does not matter that hipsters don't work. Quite frankly FeudalCare does not give a rat's ass that they don't work. It is perception that matters not reality. Hipsters make it look like FeudalCare cares, and that they are doing something to protect and prevent residents from breaking bones. Again, that is all that matters!

Immediately following Dewey Screwem and Ann Howe's meeting, CNAs are frantically going about outfitting every resident with their own personalized pair of egg cartons sewn into underwear.

The janitor and the floor washer stop their janitorial and floor washing duties, and are going about installing every conceivable alarm known to man. Bed alarms, body alarms, wheelchair alarms, you name it they are installing it. As they are in the process of installing these marvels of modern day technology, already one alarm sounds. It is Room 238; how could that be? Gert has not moved from the fetal position in 10 years. You know people, myself included who can't remember what they did from one minute to the next. Hell it is possible to pinpoint Gert's exact location and whereabouts for the last 9 years, 240 days, 17 minutes, and 6 seconds. 1t is none other than where she is right now, that damn bed of hers!

It is rather distressing, though, not to know if she was facing the window or the door. Like how many licks does it take to get to the center of a tootsie pop, the world may never know. As distraught as the janitor and the floor washer are, at having to temporarily cease installing these lifesaving mechanisms, out of love, concern, and Gert's daughter Selma's 3.2-million-dollar net worth, they go check it out. Sure enough, there is Gert as she always is, sound asleep in bed, but for some reason her bed alarm is beeping mercilessly. How could this be? Surely the brilliant janitor and his equally brilliant sidekick, the floor mopper, could not have made an installation mistake. Don Quixote and Sancho Panza never messed up, and they had nothing on these two.

Screwem and Howe only purchase alarms from the most highly reputable companies. Certainly, the company did not put out a defective alarm. Nonetheless the alarm is going off and it should not be. With a heavy heart they shut off the alarm. Curses, foiled again, as Maxwell Smart would say on the old TV show *Get Smart*. One possible explanation is that the added weight of the newly installed hipsters on Gert may have activated the alarm. Alas, all we can do is speculate.

Oh, just disconnect it, a disgusted janitor says to the visibly distraught floor mopper!

The janitor is a member of the FeudalCare team. He is not just a janitor, he is a member of MANAGEMENT because he is head of the janitorial and floor washing department. He likes to call it Environmental Control and Services. So you can imagine the shock and disbelief on the floor washer's face when he said:

Hey, Cliffy, wouldn't it be cool to pour some gin in Gert's feeding tube.

Heck ya, Norby, I remember once I blew some pot smoke in my cat's face.

That cat loved it, man, he got so buzzed and I had a blast watching him stumble around.

That's funny, Cliffy. But seriously, Gert can't walk and they could smell the pot smoke, so gin in her feeding tube would be perfect!

Yea, Norby, and it's odorless too so no one would ever know the difference.

I bet it would make Gert feel better than she has in years, Cliffy, and it is a heck of a lot cheaper and more fun than that damn morphine they pump into her.

Isn't that a crock of shit that here Gert is lying incapacitated with no quality of life and it is considered a crime to give her gin.

That's people for you, ludicrous and hypocritical,

I'll say, A dog is able to die with more dignity than a human being, it is crazy. If a dog is terminal and suffering they get put out of their misery. If a human being is terminal and suffering, they are kept alive at all costs, and made to suffer even more.

Well we can't do anything to change it so we might as well forget the whole thing.

You're right about that, but I will tell you what, gin is a hell of a lot better idea than that moron son of hers had about putting pureed salmon in her feeding tube.

Did that nitwit really say that?

Yea! I'm surprised he didn't say to throw some insulin in the blender and mix it right in with the salmon.

I wouldn't put it past him. Hell, the damn fish would get stuck in the tube. I know.

Well we better get back to work. Hey, Cliff?

Yea, Norby.

This conversation never took place, right? What conversation?

That a boy, Cliffy.

Does this mean I need to throw out the tape recorder? CUFFY!

Just kidding', Gotcha, Norby. Ha ha, very funny!

CHAPTER 3

Gert Gets Out of Bed

Janey and Rachel made a pact that they were going to be on their best behavior and not aggravate Nurse Dee Dee. Not an easy task, to say the least. The first thing the morning shift is supposed to do, is pick up the soiled linen bags in each room and toss them down the laundry shoot.

Janey, I will take the right side of the hall. No problem, Rachel, I will take the left then. Cool.

Janey, can you help me with this bag, it is really heavy.

Sure, Rachel, I would be glad to. Oh my gosh this is awfully heavy. I know, there must be weeks of dirty linen in this bag.

Well, at least we got it into the wheel barrel, now all we have to do is dump it down the laundry shoot.

Janey and Rachel pick up the remaining bags and dump them down the laundry shoot. AHHH! AHHH! AHHH! AHHH! They hear just as the bags are going down the shoot.

Rachel, where is that noise coming from?

I don't know, Janey, I think it came from down the hall.

I'II check out one room and you take the other. I think it came from one of those two rooms over there.

Sounds like a good idea.

Nothing here, Janey.

Nothing over here either, Rachel.

Well, let's go down to the laundry room and start tossing those bags into the washing machines.

Do we have to?

Yes, Rachel, we have to.

The two CNAs head down to the laundry room and commence tossing the dissolving bags into the washing machines.

Janey, can you help me with this real heavy bag again? I can't lift it by myself into the machine.

Sure, Rachel, I will be glad to. God, Janey, this is heavy.

Well, at least we got it into the machine and are done lifting it. Thank goodness.

After that workout, Janey and Rachel are extremely thirsty, so they head to the break room for a soda. As they are walking back to the laundry room to start folding clean towels and linen, they hear that scream again, AHHH! AHHH! AHHH! AHHH!

Oh no, Rachel, there is that yelling again. We better run down and check it out.

Upon entering the laundry room, the yells are louder and clearer. To make matters worse, Gert's head is bobbing up and down above a sea of soap suds.

Shit, Rachel, those goofy Aides last night must have been drunk and tossed Gert right into the soiled linen bag with the bed sheets.

Damn it, Janey, we are in deep shit. Not only is Feudal Care going to ream us a new asshole, but what about Gert's family? Gert's daughter Selma has that $3.2 million trust fund. She can afford the best lawyer and sue the hell out of us. We will lose our license too.

Don't worry, Rachel, Gert was supposed to get a shower today anyway. I'll go up to her room and get her clothes and wheelchair. You start drying her off and putting on a Depend.

Great idea, Janey, I will lock the door so no one can get in. Knock three times, not on the ceiling, but on the door.

OK.

Janey gets Gert's clothes and wheelchair with no one noticing, and successfully makes it back to the laundry room.

Good job, Janey, I got Gert dry and put on her Depend.

I'll put on her clothes, Rachel. We'll put her in the wheelchair, and no one will be the wiser.

I am glad this nightmare is almost over, Janey.

Me too. It is a good thing her muscles are so atrophied and flimsy, she didn't even get hurt. There is not a scratch on her.

We were really lucky, Janey, there is no way we could have dodged this bullet. There was no way we were going to be able to explain this not only to Screwem and Howe, but Gert's daughter Selma as well.

Unlock the door, Janey, I'll wheel Gerty out. At least we don't need to give her a shower now.

That is good news, Rachel. You know what, Janey?

What, Rachel?

We should work at the prison. Janey laughs.

No, I'm serious.

Why, Rachel?

Think about it, no pressure. What do you mean?

Well, if we accidentally threw a convict in the washing machine and he drowned, no one is going to give a shit.

Laugh again from Janey.

And, Janey, so what if we accidentally give Charles Manson an injection of cyanide instead of insulin. The public ain't gonna care. We would not get in trouble with the law or any administrative executives. Hell, we would probably be heroes.

That's true, Rachel, and Nurse Dee Dee would love us.

Why, Janey?

Are you kidding me? It is practically a prerequisite for any guy Nurse Dee Dee dates to have a felony on his resume.

I did not know that.

Yea, Rachel, this loser she is with now, Cassidy, he was allegedly in jail for murdering some guy in Mexico or something.

Is that the guy she was screwing out in the parking lot while neglecting her residents, Janey?

Well actually she screwed him after she spent an hour and a half on the clock shopping at Walmart while neglecting her residents, but ya, that's the guy, Rachel.

Wow! Well, I am sure she is just trying to rehabilitate and save the souls of these poor, unfortunate men.

Yea, that is it, Rachel, and I wanna marry Ricky Martin for his mind.

Anyway, we should apply,

Sounds good, let's check it out on our next day off, OK?

Perfect.

Great.

As they leave the laundry room and walk down the hall, whose heads do you think emerge from behind a closed door? It was none other than President Screwem and Vice President Howe.

Shit, Rachel.

1 see, Janey.

Good morning, ladies.

Good morning, President Screwem and Vice President Howe.

Morning, sir, ma'am.

What's this I see, you got Gert up and about?

Yes, sir, I hope you don't mind us taking Gert down here for a walk while we were taking care of the laundry?

Not at all, ladies, an exuberant Howe says, great idea to do the laundry and care for a resident at the same time. That is an excellent way to maximize productivity and keep our expenses low.

Thank you, ma'am. You're welcome.

Thank you, ma'am. You're welcome.

Ladies, doesn't Gert usually remain in bed, though?

Yes, President Screwem, she does, however, Rachel and I checked her chart, and she doesn't have any doctor's order restricting her to bed. We felt it would do her a world of good to get up and out of bed for a change.

Good thinking, ladies, utters V.P. Howe in her condescendingly nice voice.

Thank you, echoes Rachel.

Well, I am sure you ladies have work you need to get back to. V. P. Howe and myself need to get to a Republican Fund-raiser.

Janey and I are Republicans too.

Splendid, a beaming Screwem and Howe respond. Well, good day, ladies.

Good day, President Screwem and Vice President Howe.

Screwem and Howe head out to comfort the comfortable and afflict the afflicted.

Janey and Rachel breathe a sigh of relief.

That was close, Rachel, but we pulled it off. Yes we did, Janey, and I am quite proud.

Rachel, can you believe those two nitwits actually believed we are Republicans?

Hell, Janey, those two morons would believe we fought in the Civil War and just maintained our age well.

Im sure they would, Rachel, I am sure they would.

CHAPTER 4

Tube Free

In another hall, Wanda, age 50, is attempting to get up and go to the bathroom. This is a definite NO, NO! Wanda needs adult supervision from a CNA or Nurse for such a hazardous undertaking! Wanda is 5'4, 420 pounds. When Wanda was very young, her doctor put her on a pasteurized diet. So, any time food passed her eyes, she ate it. Lap Banding is out of the question because the band can't be taken off to pig out at Thanksgiving. Doctors are baffled as to why Wanda has severe breathing difficulty. In the weeks to come they will run a battery of tests to find out why Wanda is Oxygen-in-take challenged. Like R.P. McMurphy in *One Flew Over the Cuckoo's Nest*, she, as well as her doctors, want to get to the bottom of this problem.

Fortunately for Wanda her room overlooks the smoke hut outside. A totally stressed and burnout CNA is enjoying one of life's few pleasures, a good smoke. He just happens to glance in and notice Wanda trying to get up. Quickly he gets up, takes one last puff, and races inside to try and rescue Wanda. He gets to her room just in time to prevent Wanda from tripping over the tangled tubes of her oxygen machine. Another crisis passed. Thanks to the skill and dedication of a FeudalCare CNA, Wanda is safely rescued.

The CNA stops for a minute, catches his breath and does something a CNA rarely does, pauses to think. You know, many years ago telephones had long lines and chords. It was thought impossible for phones to operate without all those chords and wires. But, alas now we have cordless and cell phones. Why not do the same thing with oxygen machines? Let's go tubeless! Tubeless oxygen machines could be the wave of the future.

Life is already difficult enough having to be on oxygen, not to mention lugging around those cumbersome corded machines and tubes. There is no need to inflict more peril into their life with the added possibility of tripping over cords and tubes.

1 can only offer this CNA the same bit of advice Casey Casum would, keep reaching for the stars, who knows, maybe one day tubeless oxygen machines may make you a millionaire. Then you could own your own nursing home.

CHAPTER 5

Invalids Don't Walk or Like Window Cleaner

Nurse Dee Dee is one of FeudalCare's most conscientious and dedicated professionals, except on days when she does not give a shit! However, if you happen to catch Nurse Dee Dee on one of her born again virgin days, she is the consummate health care provider. Today we find Nurse Dee Dee frantically running around trying to find CNA Danielle, so she can take the temperature and get the weight of a resident who is on life supports. It is so important that a comatose resident have a few Tylenol in their system. Heaven forbid they should die with a fever and less than ideal body weight.

As if getting the temperature and weight of a man with one foot in the grave isn't important enough, Nurse Dee Dee is scared to death that a bottle of Windex was left on bedridden Minnie's dresser six feet away. She is absolutely livid and now we see her roaming the break area (where else would you find a committed FeudalCare CNA) looking for CNAs Roberta and Jimmy to reprimand them for their negligence. Upon spotting them she races over to chastise them, but not before wolfing down a plate of Nachos with Cheese. Finally, after finishing her nutritious snack, and bitching to herself about how fat she is getting, she gets around to the table where Roberta and Jimmy are sitting.

She addresses them very calmly and politely, being the consummate professional. Excuse me, Roberta and Jimmy, did you two do rounds this evening?

Why of course, Nurse Dee Dee, we always do rounds, Jimmy responds and Roberta nods in agreement.

Well, you could have fooled me.

Whatever do you mean? asks a stunned Roberta.

First off, you two were supposed to put Malcom in bed. He is up wandering the halls. The nut is on suicide watch and he probably has a gun. 1 am so sick of that man's black ass attitude. And, a bottle of Windex was left on Minnie's dresser. Didn't you check the entire room for hazards after changing Minnie?

No, Nurse Dee Dee, I am sorry, we did not, it must have slipped our minds, we do apologize, and it will not happen again, an embarrassed Jimmy answers.

Sorry does not cut it, folks, what if Minnie got out of bed and drank the Windex, it could have killed her, what would you have said to her family? Good thing I was smart enough to take it out of her room and put it back in the locked closet where it belongs.

As always you are right, Nurse Dee Dee; however, Minnie has not walked in five years, and if by some miracle she was able to start walking again, do you really think the first thing she is going to do upon regaining her mobility is to walk over to her dresser and drink a bottle of Windex? Roberta responds using every ounce of self-control she has in her body not to laugh in Nurse Dee Dee's face.

Well it could happen, and I don't like your attitude, that is not appropriate resident care, Nurse Dee Dee angrily shouts back.

You're right, Nurse Dee Dee, I swear it will never happen again, responds Jimmy, hoping he can keep a straight face for just a few moments longer until Nurse Dee Dee can get her ugly acne-scarred face the hell away from him.

Well, all right, it is a good thing I am a good Christian woman and have a lot of forgiveness in my heart, otherwise I would write you up and notify Screwem and Howe, and 1 am sure they would fire you!

Thank you, Nurse Dee Dee, says Roberta. Nurse Dee Dee? Yes, Jimmy?

May I ask you a question? Sure.

With all due respect, you being a good Christian and all.

I am the best Christian, Jimmy.

OK, then why is it all right for you say you are tired of Malcom's black ass attitude, and to tell us to be careful around him, because he is suicidal and may have a gun? But, it is not OK for Janey and Rachel to jokingly call the residents decrepit old geezers? Why is one abuse and not the other?

Because I am the Head Nurse and I say it is OK. And besides, I don't like Malcom, and I like the residents Janey and Rachel were referring to.

Thank you for clearing that up for me, Nurse Dee Dee. It is always nice to be enlightened. I think I have a better idea what it means to be a Christian now.

Wonderful, Jimmy, I am glad I could clear that up for you. So am I, Nurse Dee Dee, so am I.

Oh, and by the way, could you two stop in the kitchen and grab me a couple of ice cream bars and clock me out for lunch?

Roberta, obviously feeling uncomfortable with Nurse Dee Dee's request, asks her, Nurse Dee Dee, it says on the kitchen door that taking food is stealing and will result in termination. And, I know the handbook says it is forbidden to clock in or out for a fellow employee.

Oh, it will be OK. Don't you think?

Jimmy is a little concerned as well. Are you sure, Nurse Dee Dee?

I am the Charge Nurse, and the epitome of morality and virtue, if I say it is all right, it is all right.

You are positive it is OK, Nurse Dee Dee? Are you two questioning me?

No, ma'am.

No, ma'am.

Then do it!

Yes, ma'am.

Yes, ma'am.

CHAPTER 6

Let's Get Physical

President Screwem, V.P. Howe, dedicated Nurses like Tilly and Dee Dee are emphatic about vital signs. If a person so much as coughs, farts, sneezes, hemorrhages blood from the head, or has a limb severed, if you take vital signs, that person will be OK, and live forever.

There is no reason to take vital signs every time a resident falls. It does not accomplish shit.

Certainly, residents Bernie and Pat have fallen practically every day of their adult life walking home from taverns. Drunks Against Mad Mothers (DAMM) were certainly pleased that they walked and did not drive. Bernie and Pat are alive and kicking (well just barely) at 85. If anyone is used to falling and getting back up again it is Bernie and Pat.

Hell, Gordie and Stan played ice hockey into their 60s, tell me they didn't fall? And Blanche, she broke her leg sky diving 20 years ago when she was 73 years old.

I don't know how it is in other countries, but in addition to having the fattest youth in the world, the USA has the fattest old people. CNA Bert suggested at the last FeudalCare meeting, that we start exercising the residents more, by making them walk. CNA Andrew praised Bert for his suggestion, but politely mentioned that he has found walking to be very boring and not at all challenging, if you do it day after day. So, Andy suggested that rather than just walk, since we have so many ex-jocks and jockesses, that we have athletic competitions.

Norm, a slightly obese resident, overheard this conversation, he was waddling back to his room after going outside to smoke and grab a Pepsi and Hershey bar from the vending machines.

So immediately he commented.

I don't need to participate in any athletic activities or exercise programs. I am very active already. I watch aerobics on TV and every Sunday I watch at least two football or basketball games, so I am in good shape! If you really wanna get me in shape, you'll stick a catheter in me, so I don't have to keep getting up to pee and miss all the action. Also, while you are at it build a little refrigerator into my reclining chair so I don't have to keep getting up to get beer. That also makes me miss a lot of activity in the ball games and aerobic shows.

How is the beer going to help your health and physical fitness, Norm? Because beer is healthy for you.

How is beer healthy for you?

On the aerobic shows they are always talking about how important it is for your health and fitness to get plenty of fiber in your diet.

And how does beer do that, Norm?

You people are health professionals, I shouldn't have to tell you that, you should already know that. Haven't you ever read the label on a can of beer? It is made from barley, wheat, oats, and rye. All excellent sources of fiber.

Andy humored Norm, told him that his point was well taken, and continued verbalizing his own train of thought. He agreed to start implementing the athletic competition the following morning.

Don and Al are always fighting over bibs in the dining room, so Andy had them lace up the boxing gloves, and let them have at it in the padded room. While it was not Ali vs Frazier caliber it certainly was entertaining. And, Don and Al had a BLAST!

Unexpected good fortune arose from the Don vs Al fight as well. It turns out the lab was coming to get a blood sample from Don to run some tests. You know how important it is to make sure terminal residents don't get any new diseases before they die. Anyway, Don had a small cut over his eye that was bleeding. Nurse Dee Dee, exhibiting her heads-up nursing skills, had the wherewithal to hold a test tube under Don's eye and catch the dripping blood. The phlebotomist, upon hearing the great news that she didn't have to draw Don's blood, was thrilled.

This is great, I hate needles, they are so yucky. I just close my eyes and stab. As luck would have it, or unluck I should say, V.P. Ann Howe just happened to be paying a little visit to the humble FeudalCare facility and got wind of what was going on. She was not amused. Turns out that page 80 section 6 paragraph 4 of the FeudalCare Handbook emphatically states, if a resident so much as even attempts to hit another resident, it must be considered a full-blown punch and fall. Therefore, vital signs must be taken on both the puncher and the punchee.

It just wasn't the same the next day, when it took three hours to complete a three-minute round. The clock had to be stopped every five seconds, and over 2000 vital signs had to be taken. Nuts to that. From then on, boxing was never attempted again at the FeudalCare Nursing Home.

Well, back to the drawing board. At the next weekly shindig CNA Jason brought up the idea of tackle football. While boxing was a splendid idea till V.P. Howe turned killjoy and mandated vital signs be taken for every jab and punch, football had the advantage of allowing more participants at any given time.

Next morning two football games got started. With each team needing 11 offensive and 11 defensive players, and a total of four teams, 88 of the 100 residents got to participate at any given time. The 12 that didn't were bedridden and on life supports anyway. Hal was a little pissed because he couldn't go both ways. CNA Deron politely told Hal that no one cared about his sex life and to just be grateful he could still play at all.

One deadbeat's misfortune is another old fart's opportunity. Two CNAs were doing range of motion (rom) and stretching exercises on a resident, to limber him up for the big game. They forgot to lubricate his elbows with motor oil and his knees with WD-40. Oblivious to the resident's distress, they accidentally snapped off his limbs.

Shit, look what we did! Oh fuck!

At this point all they could do was toss the old geezer, along with his detached body parts, into the dumpster. Luckily no one was watching. I don't think anyone even noticed his absence, because not a word was mentioned. On the bright side, Hal got his wish and was able to play both offense and defense. The game went on without a hitch.

While walkers, canes, merry walkers, and wheelchairs did slow the game down a tad, it more than made up for it in improving the quality of tackles. But wouldn't you know it, just when it appeared everything was smooth sailing and football was going to be a regular weekly event at FeudalCare, "Miss Goody-Two Shoes" CNA Candi felt tackle football was abusive, and not only that but that each tackle was a fall. A fall can mean only one thing, VITAL SIGNS!

Candi did agree not to call Screwem about the alleged "abusive football" but only if it was agreed vital signs were taken after every tackle. Needless to say, this was a miserable failure.

If you thought it took long for a three-minute round of boxing every time you had to stop the clock to do vital signs, it was absolutely off the chart having to stop a 12-minute football game every 10 seconds to do vital signs.

President Screwem and Y.P. Howe finally agreed that the only sport seniors at FeudalCare could participate in was swimming. No way you can fall swimming, a very stern and business-like Director of Nursing (DON) Dianne Smells said just after returning from a sabbatical on how to get more for less out of your Nursing Staff.

One thing our two resident geniuses Screwem and Howe overlooked was the drowning potential. Apparently, this topic was not discussed at Smell's sabbatical either.

The very first day of swimming, when resident Wolfstein was lowered into the water with the crane, she sunk to the bottom of the pool quicker than spit evaporates from a hot grill. Two scared but very brave CNAs, along with one Nurse, immediately leaped into the water and attempted to rescue Wolfstein. Wolfstein would not budge. By the time the crane was reattached to Wolfstein and she was hoisted out of the pool, it was too late, Wolfstein had drowned.

Of course, it didn't help matters that they took 20 minutes before they could find anyone licensed in CPR. None of the CNAs or Nurses kept their CPR license current. Turns out the janitor and the floor mopper had to flag down a car on the highway. Miraculously it only took three attempts to find a licensed CPR expert speeding down the highway. Had CPR been performed immediately Wolfstein may have survived. We will never know!

Upon hearing about Resident Wolfstein's demise, Screwem, Howe, and Smells were deeply saddened. Not just because her rent wasn't paid up for the month, and no, not because they had to find another live old body to occupy Wolfstein's vacant bed.

No, they were deeply saddened because a fellow human being had lost her life.

Oh well, said Screwem, at least no vital signs had to be taken. We can all be thankful for that, agreed Smells.

Amen to that, sighed Howe.

An investigation is currently underway to see if, had Wolfstein been wearing hipsters, would it have provided enough of a floatation device to have kept her from drowning. If the results are conclusive, Screwem, Howe, and Smells plan to pass immediate legislation mandating the use of hipsters not only in the pool, but the bathtub and shower as well!

CHAPTER 7

Hunger Pains

In an interview with the *National Enquirer*, President Screwem said, It is all about integrity, Y.P. Howe and myself are sworn to uphold the truth, and present the facts accurately. I can emphatically say that every resident of FeudalCare enjoys a high-quality life.

After 12 years at the helm of FeudalCare Enterprises, the public still marvels at the way Screwem and Howe handle one crisis after another. Whether it is putting locks on the refrigerator to prevent employees from quenching their thirst, to cutting wages, or downgrading working conditions, the hallmark of the Screwem and Howe legacy is that they always come out on top.

The current fiasco is no exception. DON Dianne Smells was panic stricken because many of the residents were dying of starvation between the three-hour time span of one 5000 calorie meal to the next. Screwem and Howe were bound and determined to put an end to this.

So one cold, damp Friday night Screwem and Howe huddled together in Screwem's basement with a case of Grape Nehi and a bag full of Snickers candy bars. V.P. Howe turned on an old *Mr. Ed* rerun, and they got to work. Like always, Screwem and Howe were totally dedicated to get to the bottom of this.

After racking their brains for what seemed like days, (actually it was only 2 hours) and countless Grape Nehi and Snickers bars later, a light flickered on in Screwem's head. Similar to what happened to Buddha after sitting under a fig tree for 7 years. I got it, Ann, an overjoyed Screwem shouted, I don't know why I did not think of it sooner, SNACKS!! Let's supplement our high calorie, high fat meals with high calorie, high fat snacks. Surely this will end the starvation problem!

Brilliant, Dewey, brilliant, and elated Ann Howe shouted, but do you really think it will work?

I know so, retorted Screwem.

After only a few hours' sleep, a weary yet deliriously happy Screwem and Howe returned to the FeudalCare Corporate Office. Exuberant, both Howe and Screwem shouted for secretary Fanny to take a letter. Fanny did not respond right away so needless to say Screwem and Howe were slightly agitated. After a few more minutes of futile searching, Howe glanced out the window and spotted Fanny outside catching a smoke, polishing her nails, and drinking a cup of Ovaltine. Howe and Screwem momentarily longed for the good old days when secretaries could keep an ashtray right at their desk and smoke in the office. Sure, our clothes and office stunk, but goddammit, productivity was double back then than what it is now.

They motion for Fanny to get inside and take a letter. Fanny hustles in, sits down, spills her Ovaltine, gets up to retrieve some paper towels, and cleans up the spill. Finally, she is ready to take a letter.

Dewey starts dictating, to all honorable and distinguished staff at FeudalCare, itis after much deliberation between myself and V.P. Howe, that we feel we have come up with the solution to our starvation problem. Medical Science will back me up when I say that three hours between 5000 calorie meals is way too long for a body to go without food. No wonder we've had so many deaths at FeudalCare due to starvation. Effective immediately we are implementing a mandatory snack program. Every hour our residents must be force-fed high calorie, high fat snacks to supplement their high calorie, high fat meals. Potato chips, doughnuts, cheese curls and sodas are all to be pushed. I realize that some residents will shove the snacks away, saying they are too full. Don't believe it for a minute, they are not lucid enough to make such an important decision as to whether they are hungry or not. Their lives are far too important to us. L fneed be, mix the snacks in a plastic bag and give them to them intravenously. Their very lives may depend on it, and their families will be grateful for our life-saving efforts.

To all kitchen staff, please be sure to increase snack orders by tenfold, and to all admissions people, please increase the monthly rent by $1000.

Off the record, Screwem winks and nudges Howe and says, No reason we can't make a few extra bucks for ourselves with our humanitarianism.

Sincerely yours in Christ, Dewey Screwem

President of FeudalCare Enterprises

The program was a huge success, only one resident died from a food related injury that year. It appears that either one Aide went a little overboard stuffing food into a resident's mouth, or the resident simply gorged himself to death, and he exploded. V.P. Howe reminded President Screwem to keep his head held high.

Let's not dwell on the negatives, Dewey, rather be positive, no one died from starvation, and the one unfortunate exploding incident, at least no vital signs had to be taken! This program has been a real blessing to our census, it has remained at 98% capacity the entire year. That is unprecedented, Dewey. Yes indeed, Ann, the program sure makes senses to us! And our wallets!

CHAPTER 8
Too Much TLC

It was CNA Kitty's first day on the job. She was 18, just graduated high school and had spent the last four months touring Europe. Kitty's old man was loaded; he had invested heavily into the prophylactic and rubber glove industry 20 years ago at the beginning of the AIDS epidemic kicked off by Rock Hudson. Kitty's allergy to latex prompted him to develop a whole line of latex free plastic gloves as well. Sure, enough this endeavor netted him a fortune, as he surmised correctly, there are literally millions upon millions of unfortunate souls like Kitty who are also burdened with latex intolerance.

Kitty was always a caring and compassionate person and wanted to get into the healthcare industry. As a kid, she was always bringing home stray cats and dogs. A friend suggested she get licensed as a CNA, this would provide her with excellent training and experience for a career as a Nurse, a lifelong ambition of Kitty's.

Kitty was counting on DON Dianne Smells to give her a good recommendation to Liver Sea School of Nursing. Being a very dedicated and hardworking girl, Kitty felt certain she would be accepted. That, and her dad's $1,000,000 donation to the school.

Kitty's first day on the job was incredibly traumatic for her, but a huge source of giggles for her trainer and her coworkers. Kitty was casually sitting in her chair being briefed about various procedures and aspects of the job. After going over the fundamentals of the job, Kitty and her coworker, the one who was training her, engaged in some small talk about each other's lives and just generally chewed the fat. Suddenly, a light went off. Kitty freaked out, she leapt from her chair and ran as fast as she could to the room where the light was going off. She figured her coworker would be right behind her, but she wasn't. Maybe she stopped to get CPR equipment, Kitty thought. After a minute or so, when still no coworker showed up, Kitty grew frantic. Maybe another emergency popped up that she needed to attend to first. Maybe she got hurt and was not able to make it to the room. Kitty hauled ass back to the desk. Kitty did not see Lacey her trainer behind the station, but saw two other CNAs laughing it up and having a good old time.

Where is Lacey? Kitty shouted.

1 don't know, responded one of the other CNAs, 1 think she went to get a soda.

Get a soda? a hysterical Kitty said, how could she, a light is going off.

The other two CNAs looked at Kitty, then looked at each other in shock disbelief, like Kitty was a raving lunatic.

What is the matter with you people? Kitty screamed, almost in tears. You two are laughing and Lacey is getting a soda, can't you see a light is going off? Yea, so what? said one of the CNAs, lights goof of all the time, it's no big deal.

No big deal!

By now you could see that Kitty was visibly shaken. She thought to herself, Do I really want to work in a profession where CNAs are so callous about another human beings' life that they won't stop goofing around to answer a light?

Finally, Kitty cried, that lady could be dying, and you all just sit there and laugh.

The other two Aides thought Kitty was joking around and started laughing. Just as they were about to praise Kitty for her sense of humor, it became abundantly clear that Kitty was not joking around and that she was dead serious. They stopped laughing and looked a little sheepish.

Dying, one of them said, what in the world are you talking about?

Room 147 pulled the light, she must be having a heart attack, stroke, or a serious fall.

What in the world ever gave you that idea, Kitty? said a soda-sipping Lacey back from the break room.

I thought the light was strictly for emergencies, Kitty said, like a fire alarm, that you only pull in life or death situations.

Mrs. Jackson, a 20-year CNA veteran, on light duty from cramps and water retention, just happened to hear Kitty's remark as she walked by to grab a copy of *Soap Digest*. Bless your heart, honey child, you poor thing, are you naive! That light is not for emergencies at all, it is for room service, i.e. changing a TV channel, turning a page of a book, lighting a cigarette, mixing a martini, etc.

Please let it be known that FeudalCare is fastidious about law and order, they would never let a CNA under the age of 16 light a cigarette for a resident, or anyone under the age of 21 mix an alcoholic beverage.

Unfortunately, Kitty, although very intelligent like all CNAs are, was very immature and unable to laugh at herself. She felt totally humiliated and embarrassed by everyone laughing at her mis-perception.

That is not funny, she cried as she stamped her feet and pouted like a 10- year-old spoiled brat, not being allowed to stay up late at night and watch *Family Guy*. You wait and see, I am going to tell my mommy, I mean President Screwem, you'll see, you'll all be sorry.

The thought of having to endure the wrath of Screwem chilled every snickering CNA to the bone. We are sorry, the suddenly remorseful and somber CNAs all said in unison, it will never happen again, we promise, please don't tell President Screwem. He will write us up, or even worse yet, send us to timeout.

Well, you should have thought about that before you ridiculed and humiliated me, a spoiled Kitty whined back, acting like a two-year-old. Kitty immediately took out her cell phone and called her mom to have Maurice the chauffeur come pick her up. She refused to be treated in such an undignified manner.

Back home, Kitty's mom and dad tried to comfort their "little pumpkin" as the butler brought out lady fingers and Kool- aid to console her. After mom and dad lifted the spirit of their "little angel" and Kitty daintily finished her snack, Kitty went out to the barn to ride her horse Lucky.

That warm spring afternoon, FeudalCare lost a wonderful CNA and potentially outstanding Nurse, but it was no skin off Kitty's teeth, she still had her horse Lucky, and Daddy's trust fund!

In the midst of all the haste and confusion, Kitty accidentally donned a pair of latex gloves. That evening her whole body swelled up like a stuffed sausage. She passed away shortly after midnight.

FeudalCare decided it was best for the business and the morale of the staff to hide the obituary and just let everyone get on with their lives. Fortunately for Kitty, since she quit prior to her demise, President Screwem and V.P. Howe did not need a Doctor's Note excusing her absence.

CHAPTER 9

Laughing at Yourself

It is 9:45 p.m., time for CNA Ray to get his fat, lazy ass out of bed and get ready to work the IO p.m. shift at FeudalCare. At I 0:15 p.m. he emerges from the shower and commences dressing. At I 0:20 p.m. his wife Samantha is screaming at him. You can tell she is mad, it takes a lot to interrupt her from yelling at the kids for losing the TV remote control, that she is sitting on. In all fairness to Samantha, though, she really does lose her car keys. And send you upstairs to get her purse when she left it downstairs. Samantha is also a certified expert on every aspect of driving, provided she is either in the passenger or back seat. She has no qualms about waking you up out of a sound sleep to have you get something for her.

Get your ass out the door, Raymond, or you are going to get fired. I've been doing this for three years, they ain't gonna fire me.

It is going to catch up with you. You can't just show up to work 45 minutes late every day and expect to keep a job, Raymond.

No one ever calls him Raymond. Except for his mom when she is angry with him. Like when he was little and ate the neighbor's daisies, and like she stills does for not being a devout Episcopalian.

You better not stop for coffee, Raymond, his wife shouts as he walks out the door and locks it behind him.

Yea, yea, he mumbles to himself walking to the car. He pulls out of the driveway and goes about a half mile down the road and turns back. Shit! I forgot my book bag, he shouts. By now they are all freaking out at the old folks' home, thinking Raymond is not coming in tonight, and they are going to be shorthanded.

He gets back home, and Samantha is furious to hear the door open and see him walk through.

What is it now? she demands. I forgot my duffle bag.

You don't need that goddamn duffle bag, get to work, you asshole. Yea, I know.

If you get fired, so help me, Raymond, you can just pick up your things and leave, you have a family to support, you need to be more responsible.

Yea I know.

Raymond picks up his duffle bag and heads out the door, but not before startling the dogs, who in turn bark, wake up the kids and give Samantha another reason to go off into a tirade. Raymond finally heads off to work again but not before stopping at the 7-11 first to get coffee. He gets a large black coffee and shoots the breeze for a few minutes with the 7-11 employees. He has been in there every day, twice a day, five days a week, for the last three years, so down at the old 7-11, they know Raymond pretty well.

Raymond heads off to work finally, but about 3/4 of the way there, he turns around and heads back home to make sure the door is locked. He gets back home, and parks about 200 feet from the house, so Samantha won't know he is back again by the car lights shining through the window.

Just as I thought, the door is locked, but you can never be too sure, I better go around and check the back door again too, even though I know it is locked.

Raymond sprints to the back door. I better run, he thinks to himself, I need to save time and get to work as soon as possible. The back door is definitely locked, I know so because I have marked it down on a sheet of paper 13 times, THE DOOR IS DEFINITELY LOCKED!

He sprints back to the car, remember, he is in a hurry and needs to save time, to get to work as soon as possible. He leaps back in the car and for a 3" time heads to work. Well as everyone knows by now, President Screwem and V.P. Howe run a very tight ship at FeudalCare. You have to get up very early in the morning to "pull the wool over their eyes." It happens, but it is extremely rare if someone is an hour late and they don't notice. Quickly Nurse Gretel is on the phone to Raymond's home to check on his status.

Hello, ma'am, this is Gretel the overnight Nurse at FeudalCare. I hate to disturb you so late at night but Raymond is scheduled to work tonight, and he is not here yet. I was wondering if it was possible that he overslept or his alarm did not go off. Is he on his way? Samantha played dumb, obviously something she is very good at, because she married Raymond in the first place.

Gee I don't know, Samantha said, I fell asleep downstairs on the sofa watching *Revenge of the Nerds*, hold on a minute and let me run up to the bedroom and check and see if he is still here. Samantha holds the phone and silently counts to 30 and puts the phone to her mouth again. No, he is not home and his car is gone too, so he definitely left for work.

OK, Nurse Gretel says, I hope he shows up pretty soon, we are really shorthanded.

I understand, says Samantha, I am really sorry he is not there yet, I am sure he will be there pretty soon.

I hope so, says Gretel, do you think he is OK? I hope so, says Samantha, now I am worried.

I am sure he is OK, Gretel says, I will have him call you as soon as he gets in, to put your mind at ease.

I appreciate that, goodbye. Goodbye.

Immediately Samantha hangs up the phone and angrily dials Raymond on his cell phone.

Raymond was indeed heading to work, when he saw an attractive woman smoking a cigarette. He immediately pulls into the parking lot and parks the car near the payphone and, for a few minutes, pretends he is cleaning out his car, then he goes inside to buy a can of diet Coke. He comes back just in time to see the pretty girl get off the payphone, while still smoking her cigarette. Damn! She looks so hot smoking, he thinks to himself, and before you can bat an eye, mutters back to himself, I wish that girl would not smoke, it is bad for her health.

Excuse me, ma'am, do you need a ride home.

No thank you, the woman says, as she takes the last puff of her cigarette and extinguishes it with her shoe on the ground, my boyfriend is on his way to pick me up, but thank you for asking, that was very sweet of you.

You are welcome, no problem. I wonder if her boyfriend smokes, Raymond thinks to himself as he climbs back into his car. Just then his cell phone rings.

Hello?

Don't hello me, you asshole, where are you? Why aren't you at work yet?

You better not have stopped for coffee.

No, no, I didn't, Raymond nervously tells his wife, I had a flat tire of all things, and I just finished changing it.

Did you ever hear of a thing called a cell phone, why didn't you call work and tell them?

Tongue in cheek, Raymond replies, I could not find my cell phone anywhere, and it was not until you called that I heard it ring.

What about a payphone, dip shit?

I was stranded too far away from a payphone to call, so I just started changing the flat.

Well just call work and tell them.

OK, bye, honey, I love you, I will see you in the morning. Click.

Raymond hits his speed dial and calls his daughter Ruthy's cell phone. Hello, this is Ruthy.

Hi, Ruthy, thank goodness you answered the phone and it wasn't your mom.

Daddy, what are you doing, why are you calling me this late, is everything OK?

Where is your mother?

She is in your bedroom reading, is everything OK? Everything is fine, honey, did she hear the phone ring?

No, lucky for you, I had it on vibrate, otherwise Mom would have your ass in a sling.

It already is, honey, it already is. What did you call for?

Shit, I forgot.

Daddy?

Oh yea, can you check the den and make sure I shut off the heating pad?

Daddy, we go through this every night, I saw you shut it off before you left, I wanna go to sleep, I got school in the morning.

I know, honey, I am sorry, please humor me and go check, but don't let your mother hear you, OK?

OK.

Yes, Daddy, the heating pad is turned off, and it is rolled up with the chord around it sitting on the coffee table.

Great, Ruthy, thank you so much, your mother did not hear you did she? Yea, she heard me.

Oh shit.

Don't worry, Daddy, I told her! left my math book in there and that l also wanted a drink of water from the cooler because it is coldest in there.

Great, and she bought it? Yes, Daddy.

And she can't hear you talking on the phone9

I've been whispering the whole time, Daddy, and she is in your room. She didn't hear your phone ring?

It's on vibrate like I already told you.

ls my library book on the coffee table, too? Yes, it is, Daddy, why aren't you at work?

1 am at work. Thanks, sweety, go to bed and 1'11 see you in the morning.

It's gonna be morning pretty soon if you don't hang up the phone, and let me go to bed.

OK, OK, I'm sorry, honey. Good night, Ruthy. Good night, Daddy.

I love you.

I love you, too.

Bye.

Bye.

Raymond hangs up and starts pondering. 1 am very forgetful, **1** better make a note to remind myself to put the spare tire on the car in the morning and puncture a hole in the regular tire. Damn 1 wish 1 could just tell Samantha I stopped by Al's Service Station right after work, but she knows Al does not open that early. Oh well.

Raymond immediately phones FeudalCare with his bullshit excuse.

Hello, Gretel, this is Raymond, listen, I just called to apologize for being so late. I got a flat tire on the way to work, and wouldn't you know it, I pulled off the road in the worst possible place, surrounded by a huge puddle of mud, it was just an absolute mess changing it. I am so frustrated and angry right now. I know how fortunate I am to have a job at FeudalCare, and you guys have treated me with so much loyalty, I hate to be late and inconvenience you like this.

Don't be silly, Raymond, thank God you are OK. I was worried sick something happened to you. You are one of our best employees, Raymond, (Raymond puts his hand over the phone so Gretel can't hear him snicker and say, boy what a moron) did you get the tire fixed?

Even by Raymond's standard, he knows he has fucked around long enough and it really is time to get to work.

Oh yes, Gretel, I am on my way, I will be to work in a few minutes, the tire is changed. Raymond hangs up his cell phone and drives on to FeudalCare. He pulls into the FeudalCare parking lot, and because he is a creature of habit, he pulls right up to the door, leaps out with the car still running, and races through the door to the time clock and punches in. Only then does he realize his effort was in vane because he is already a gazillion hours late. At least he was sure he punched in, he read his name four times as it came upon the clock and ran his time card through the clock again five times, to see the "already punched in" code.

Raymond was a master at outfoxing Screwem and Howe. On more than one occasion, he would have a coworker punch in for him right at IO p.m., or he would tell Nurse Gretel he forgot to punch in and have her sign a missed punch form, stating that he started work at 10 p.m. No, the Nurses never questioned him, they were way too busy dealing with life and death matters, like rounding up a posse to go out and smoke, and being righteously indignant about how lousy the Nurses from the previous shift were. On more laid-back days, the Nurses would shop at Walmart or do the nasty in their boyfriends' car. Kind of high schoolish huh? Well, that is FeudalCare's finest!

Finally, Raymond is present and accounted for in the FeudalCare facility. First thing he does is head for the break room for a soda and popcorn for himself and Jacintha his co-worker for the shift. Raymond is not into self-torture; no way is he going to watch a three-hour movie on an empty stomach.

Raymond is fortunate not to be as dumb as he looks. On the other hand, he is not anywhere near as clever as he thinks he is. On more than one job, he has been referred to as the smartest dumb guy in the world, and the smartest poverty-stricken man in the world. 1fever there was an example of a square in a round peg it would be Raymond.

Handing Jacintha the soda and popcorn he begins, I am so sorry, Jacintha, it was really rude and inconsiderate of me to show up two hours late. I feel terrible that you had to fake the vital signs, weights, and do all the charting by yourself. And, to make matters worse, you had to be finished by 11:30 p.m.

Oh, don't worry about it, Raymond, it is no big deal.

Well, it is a big deal, I am going to make it up to you and hide all the Ted hose, Gerry-sleeves, and hipsters in the bottom of the dirty linen barrel myself.

Cool, that works out perfect, I don't mind faking vitals and weights, but I hate hiding all that "old people stuff"

Great, because I am just the opposite, I hate faking vitals and weights, but I don't mind disposing of the "old people stuff."

Oh, Raymond, I almost forgot to tell you, poor Mrs. Coffee passed away last night, the poor thing is finally out of her suffering. Anyway, we got pretty close and you know how she hated Nurse Dee Dee?

Yea, I remember, Jacintha.

Well she knew she was dying and did not have much time left. Yea.

She knew what a religious hypocrite Nurse Dee Dee was, so she told me as soon as she dies, to tell Nurse Dee Dee that I locked and shut all the windows and doors, so her spirit would be trapped and not be able to get up to heaven!

Oh My God, what happened?

Nurse Dee Dee freaked. She screamed at me, and ran down the hall frantically opening every window and door within eye shot. She swore she was going to tell Screwem and Howe and get me fired.

Are you worried? No.

Why not?

I told her to go ahead and tell Screwem and Howe, then I would just have to tell them about the time she told me in front of two residents about the time she was arrested for prostitution and snorted so much cocaine she thought she was going to have a heart-attack!

That is hysterical, Jacintha, too funny. What did Nurse Dee Dee do? Well, she had a terrified look on her face, and said well, I suppose I can drop the incident then.

I said, thank you, Nurse Dee Dee.

Between gritted teeth, she said you are welcome! That is just too good, Jacintha.

I know, Raymond.

Screwem and Howe were really cracking down on tardiness as of late, regardless of extenuating circumstances, so Raymond was paid a little visit in the morning. Acting like he was Albert Einstein or Plato, Screwem gave Raymond the old company line this week: If you are on time you are late. Raymond was surprised Howe didn't try to one up Ben Franklin's: A penny saved is a penny earned, with: The customer is always right.

Raymond always appreciated Screwem and Howe's fatherly and motherly advice, he really did.

Thank you for pointing out the tardy thing to me. I'm going to buckle down and behave myself. 1 don't want to get fired, because there is no way I would ever be able to get another job again if I lost this one. I don't want to have to panhandle in the streets!

Splendid, my boy, you have a wonderful attitude. You are man enough to admit you made a mistake and not only that, you are repentant.

It takes a big person to admit you are wrong, Raymond, I could not be prouder of you if I was your own mother.

Thank you, President Screwem and V.P. Howe.

You are welcome, son.

CHAPTER 10

Why Don't You Want to Work for Me?

No rest for the wicked, in the elder industry it is one crisis after another. Just when it looked like Screwem and Howe were going to get a little break after solving the starvation problem, up pops another fiasco. Seems like employee retention at FeudalCare amongst CNAs is at an all-time low. Howe is mystified by these phenomena.

Gee, I wonder why that is?

I'll be damned if I know, Ann, grumbled Screwem in his gruff voice, I just don't understand what people want, FeudalCare can give a CNA everything they want out of life.

I know, sighs the soft-spoken Howe, but don't worry, Dewey, like always we will get to the bottom of this dilemma, and FeudalCare will emerge stronger than ever.

You really think so, Ann?

I know so, Dewey.

Good, I feel better already.

Meanwhile, far removed from the ivory towers and the land of Grape Nehi and Snickers, CNAs Eric and Heidi are getting ready for round one of bed checks. Eric leaps off the sofa and pauses *Teenage Mutant Ninja Turtles*.

Heidi groans, Goddammit, I don't wanna check these old fucks, let's hurry up and get this shit over with.

Eric is the first to step into the hallway and unexpectedly slips in feces and urine, where Stu, one of the nut-bag residents, relieved himself on the floor. He slips, he slides, and just when it looks like he is going to wind up right on his ass, he reaches out at the last minute and saves himself, by grabbing on to the railing. Heidi breaks out laughing.

Feeew that was close, Eric, you almost wound up on your butt.

Goddammit, these old people are so fucking disgusting. I ought to staple gun that SOB's diaper to his ass, so he can't keep taking it off, and shitting and pissing on the floor.

I thought you loved every resident like they were a member of your own family, Eric.

That was before I almost fell in shit and piss, Eric barks back disgustedly. Eric wipes off his shoes with some wet wipes, tosses them in the trash, washes his hands and he and Heidi walk into the first room, to check on the deadbeats. First room is A-OK, both residents are asleep and dry. Ditto for the second room. Roger and Cecilia don't need to be checked. As usual Roger is ridiculing his wife.

You don't need oxygen, Cecilia, you use it as a crutch. It is mind over matter. If you'd just make up your mind that you don't need it you won't.

Nothing unusual in the third room, both residents are wet but asleep, so Eric and Heidi change them. Next room they walk in is a private room, Renee rooms by herself. Even if Renee's son didn't own the most successful strip club in town, and was not loaded, Renee would still need to room by herself.

She has a habit of clubbing innocent people sleeping with her cane. Eric opens the door and startles Renee; she screams.

You children have a lot of nerve barging in here and frightening a young girl half to death. I was just making some fresh homemade Christmas Cookies for my newborn babies.

Renee, it is the middle of July, and you don't have newborn babies, your children are 55 years old, Eric informs her.

You are crazy, I gave birth to them just last week, for heaven's sake. I should know, they are my own children.

Politely, Heidi asks her how a newborn baby can eat Christmas cookies.

Don't get smart with me, young lady, I will put you over my knee and give you a wallop. Just for that, I am not going to let you two lick the beaters.

Eric tells her, Renee, there are no beaters, there's not even a stove, you did not make Christmas Cookies.

Get out of here before I call the police, you demons, get out or I will scream.

Heidi comments on how lucid Renee is today.

I'll say, says Eric, she has not been this with-it since Lincoln gave the Gettysburg address. On the way out of Renee's room, Heidi stoops down and picks up a plastic daisy laying on the floor and hands it to Renee. Here you go, Renee, here is some flour to make some more cookie dough.

On to the next room, where lunatic Veronica is lying in bed repeating over and over, I need assistance, I need assistance, I need assistance. Veronica looks like the Grinch who stole Christmas and talks like Cruella Deville.

Her roommate Margo is sitting in her rocking chair, swaying back and forth. Margo acts like she is three sheets to the wind, more so than a crazy person. No, you don't need assistance, you need to shut your goddamn mouth and go to sleep, says Margo.

Monica, age 92 and a retired nurse, is out in the hallway chastising her sixyear-old daughter about skipping school.

You are not staying home today, young lady, you are perfectly fine, your pedal (foot) pulse is normal and your eyes are PERR LA (pupils' equal round reactive to light accommodating).

A chair gets knocked over in the dining room so Eric and Heidi go check it out. They find Melvin standing by the open refrigerator smearing cantaloupe all over his head.

What are you doing, Melvin? asks Heidi.

My doctor says my hair turned gray because it lost all its melon.

How is rubbing cantaloupe all over your head going to fix that, Melvin? I am putting melon in my hair to get the color back.

We had to ask, Heidi. I know, Eric.

While you are at it, Melvin, why don't you trim the corns off your feet to use as a vegetable?

Don't encourage him, Eric.

Let's get him cleaned up and back to bed, so we can finish this round. I'm with you, Heidi.

Room 1700A finds old man Henry sitting by his roommate Devin's bed. He is holding Devin's hand, who is sound asleep. Henry keeps repeating, I am so sorry, Dad, I did not mean it. I am here for you now, everything is going to be OK. I love you, Dad, I will never let you down again.

Suddenly old lady Glenda walks into the room. Henry looks up still holding Devin's hand. Is that old lady my mother?

I am not your mother, I am a college girl at McPherson State. Are you a sorority girl, Glenda? Heidi inquires.

Well, yes, I am.

Cool, says Eric, may I come to one of your keg parties, Glenda?

I should say not, we have high standards, we wouldn't invite the likes of you.

In the hallway Stu is walking around again, and while he is not relieving Himself on the floor this time, he is flinging soiled and wet Depends out of the trash. Heidi yells, Stu, what in the world are you doing?

What does it look like I am doing for Christ's sake. I am fixing the air conditioner, it is hotter than hell in here.

Stu, you are not fixing any air conditioner, you are making a gross mess. You people are fucking nuts, any moron can see that the air conditioner is broken and I am fixing it, goddamn it. What the hell is wrong with you people?

The call light is on in the room across the hall. Decrepit old Nellie needs to go to the bathroom for the 20th time in the last two hours.

Heidi, what Nellie really needs, is a toilet seat glued to her ass. Or a cork shoved up her butt to stop pooping.

You would think that even at age 93, walking 16 miles a day to the toilet would have Nellie's body fit and solid as a rock, but such was not the case. Eric pulls down Nellie's Depend and sits her on the toilet.

If I have to look at one more fat old lady's wrinkled ass, I am going to vomit, says Heidi, assisting Eric with Nellie.

In the room adjacent to the aforementioned room, Harold has totally peed the bed, even though he was completely changed two hours ago and two disposable pads were placed underneath him.

God, how can old people pee so much, both Heidi and Eric say in unison. Eric and Heidi work together so often, they are Like Regis and Kelly, they invariably know what the other is thinking or going to say. Even though they quite often say the same thing at exactly the same time, it still cracks both of them up, every time they do it. Immediately after taking care of Harold, Nellie needs to go to the bathroom again.

Jesus Christ, Eric yells, these people have shit and pissed over a I 00,000 times in their life. All right already, you don't need to shit or piss anymore, stop, enough is enough, the thrill should be long gone by now. Heidi and Eric are very perplexed by what they see in the next room.

Sweetheart, asks Eunice, could you take my temperature, I believe I am running a fever.

Hmmmm, Eric says, it is very unusual for someone to be hot in the middle of July, with a sun-lamp shining in their face and 16 blankets on.

Unlikely, responds Heidi, but I suppose anything is possible, Eric. Meanwhile, 99-year-old demented Harriet walks out into the hall and tells Eric and Heidi, I hope to God when I get old 1 won't be crazy like these people, as she dusts each resident's door with her hand for the 100th time in the last 24 hours.

Dodi is livid that her roommate needs her incontinent pad changed. Just let her lie there in pee, she says. These goddamn old people need to get off their asses and go to the toilet themselves the lazy bastards will never learn if you keep changing them, she says as she stands there with a dripping wet Depend.

Eric and Heidi have to be the two unluckiest people on the face of the earth. I swear to God, that if their spouses got cut in two they would get the top half. Mrs. Gladys Krapitz was visiting her husband Lenny, and heard every one of their comments about the residents. She was furious and did what any good Christian, and our Lord and Savior Jesus Christ, would have done. She immediately picked up the Red FeudalCare Bitch Line and phoned Screwem and Howe about Eric and Heidi's atrocious behavior.

It was after hours, but you can be rest assured Mrs. Krapitz left a very detailed and accurate description of Eric and Heidi's atrocious behavior. The following morning Eric and Heidi were phoned to come into the FeudalCare corporate office and talk to Screwem and Howe. Eric was about to phone Heidi, to see if she got "the call," but before he could hit Heidi's name on the speed dial, his phone rang. Heidi beat him to the punch, and she did indeed receive "the call." The two of them were summoned to meet Screwem and Howe at 1400 hours. Heidi agreed to pick up Eric at 1200 hours not only so they could stop at Denny's for lunch, but also so Heidi could show Eric her new "DON'T CHOOSE LIFE, MY MOM DID, IT SUX" bumper sticker.

Heidi pulled up to Eric's place and beeped the horn. She leaped out of the car upon seeing Eric emerge from his house, and immediately raced him to the back of her car to look at the bumper sticker.

That is great, an ecstatic Eric said, where did you get it at? I got it at my RC Meeting.

RC Meeting, what's that? Recovering Christians.

Well it is awesome, Heidi, I love it.

Thanks, I thought you would. It still isn't as good as your "NURSE DEE DEE IS THE PERFECT REASON FOR ABORTION" bumper sticker.

Yea, but this will really boil the blood of all those assholes with Bush/ Cheney bumper stickers on their cars, spewing out chunks of coal from the exhaust pipe.

Heidi and Eric get back in the car, still chuckling over the bumper sticker. They both enjoy a delicious Grand Slam meal at Denny's and hop back into the car. It is still early so they decide to pull into a convenience store for coffee. They decide to be nice and get a box of doughnuts for Nurse Dee Dee, she hasn't started her diet yet. And a pack of Salem Lights for Dr. McKenna, he used to smoke Camel filter-less, but losing that left lung scared the shit out of him so he switched to filtered smokes. If he loses the right lung, he will have no other alternative than to resort to chewing tobacco. Eric and Heidi get their coffee and head back to the car. They pull up to the office at 1350 hours and take the long walk of shame toward Screwem and Howe's office. As they approach, the door is open, Screwem and Howe, masters of the universe that they are, are sitting in the conference room smoking Cohiba cigars and sipping brandy from a snifter. They see Eric and Heidi approaching and motion for them to sit down. Screwem and Howe stand up, shake hands with Heidi and Eric, and exchange pleasantries.

President Screwem begins, Eric and Heidi, do you know why V.P. Howe and myself have called you in here today? Both Eric and Heidi feign puzzled expressions and simultaneously shrug their shoulders in unison.

Howe responds, Well, President Screwem and myself received some very disturbing news on the customer service line this morning, and let me just say, that we are none too happy about it. Do you recall anything either of you may have inferred directly or indirectly last night? Again, Eric and Heidi look at each other and shrug their shoulders in unison, both trying not to laugh at the huge booger hanging out of the nostril of President Screwem, and V.P. Howe's unzipped slacks.

President Screwem continues, Mrs. Krapitz was visiting her dear sweet in-firmed husband Lenny last night, and it appears the two of you made some very vicious and unchristian remarks about our residents last night. Do I need to repeat some of the remarks Mrs. Krapitz alleged?

No, that won't be necessary, Eric pipes up. Why not? interjects V.P. Howe.

Because we did not say anything inappropriate, said Heidi.

Goddamn it, 1 don't want to check these old fucks is not inappropriate? a shocked Screwem shouts back.

That old lady is nuttier than a fruitcake, we would never say anything like that, we love these residents, we treat them like members of our own family, says Eric.

Heidi thinks to herself, no we don't, Eric, we don't beat members of our own family. Then out loud she says, if it were not for these residents we would not have a job.

That is right, Screwem proudly interjects. I invented that saying and had it put on that plaque right over there hanging on the wall.

That is very nice, sir. Beautiful, says Heidi.

Why would Mrs. Krapitz say you said those things then? says Howe.

That woman is delusional, the other day she said that Jackie Gleason was going to have a hot fudge sundae with her and Lenny for dessert next week. She is a moron, too, insists Heidi, she thinks the New Deal is a Big Mac, a Large Fry, and a Coke.

You and Heidi seem to be using some very derogatory remarks describing her right now, Screwem points out.

You are right, President Screwem and V.P. Howe, the language we just used to describe Mrs. Krapitz is very rude and inappropriate. I apologize, it is just that Heidi and myself are visibly shaken by these allegations, none of it is true, our feelings are hurt, we are human, too, that is why we flew off the handle a little bit. But, we would never complain about taking care of the residents, President Screwem and V.P. Howe, they are not an interruption to our business, they are the reason for our business.

That is right, agrees Howe, I got that printed on my business cards right over here, see that?

Very impressive, ma'am.

Indeed, agrees Heidi.

Screwem pauses for a minute then begins to speak. Maybe Mrs. Krapitz is paranoid, obviously you two are very committed to the residents and the health care industry. That is evident by the fact that both of you knew the three Cardinal Virtues of the FeudalCare creed, only dedicated CNAs would know those by heart.

Thank you, sir.

Very much appreciated, echoes Heidi.

All right then, let's wrap this meeting up, V.P. Howe and myself are meeting with Reverend Jeremy Fakewell and Patty Roberson to discuss ways of bringing Our Lord and Savior Jesus Christ more into our everyday mission at FeudalCare. Both Eric and Heidi utilized their years of being in the Drama Club in High School, to blow smoke up Screwem and Howe's ass. Eric played Romeo and Heidi played Dorothy in the *Wizard of Oz*. Tears started to stream down their cheeks.

That is beautiful, President Screwem and V.P. Howe, I have so much respect and admiration for you two, putting your focus on the Lord.

A sniffling Heidi agreed with Eric's sentiments I 00 percent.

Screwem and Howe were so moved and touched by Eric and Heidi's sentiments that they began to well up with tears themselves. They all engaged in a group hug and blubbered like a bunch of babies.

Oh yea, before the Honorable Reverends Fakewell and Roberson get here, can either of you tell me why FeudalCare has such a difficult time retaining CNAs? Turnover is at an all-time high and neither myself nor President Screwem can figure out why.

You guys are too soft on us, you coddle us too much, pointed out Heidi. Hmmmmmmmmmmmmm, very interesting, what exactly do you mean, please expound on those sentiments for myself and V.P. Howe.

Eric took over. CNAs are very driven and intelligent people. We like to be challenged, when we are not, we get bored, lazy, lose our focus, and wind up quitting.

Interesting, very interesting, do you have any suggestions for myself and President Screwem?

Heidi picked up the ball. Well, for one, Nurses need to be like a great football coach, for example Mike Ditka, and push us on to victory and excellence.

How so? asks Screwem.

I was on the girls' gymnastic team in high school and we hated to run sprints, and none of us would do it unless the coach pushed us, even though we knew running sprints was important.

Same with the guys on my wrestling team. It is the same way with CNAs. We don't like to do vital signs, pass ice, stock diapers, wipes, wash wheelchairs, or sweep and mop the floor. Even though deep down we know it is of the utmost importance.

And, said Heidi, it is important that we start the minute we walk in the door, before we get a soda, smoke a cigarette, get a snack, etc. Otherwise, our skills just wither away. The Nurses have to be on us like ugly on an ape and stink on shit, so we get this done.

I would like to point out also, Heidi, that it is important that the Nurses follow up on us, to make sure we not only get the job done, but get it done correctly, that way we won't lose our edge or our focus.

Excellent, excellent, a delighted Screwem beams, anything else?

Oh yea, says Eric, don't let the Nurses allow us to settle down and watch TV or a movie.

And one other thing before I forget, says Heidi. Would it be OK if we stay? late or come in on our day off to help feed the residents so we can get to know them better as human beings?

Would it be OK? It would be more than OK, it would be fabulous.

Wonderful, chimes in Howe, absolutely wonderful, especially since we aren't paying you.

That's great. Heidi and myself, as well as a lot of the other CNAs we talked with, would love to do that but we did not know if it was OK or not, and we were afraid to ask.

Why were you afraid to ask myself and V.P. Howe?

You know, says Heidi, sometimes the fear of rejection is so strong, it paralyzes you from asking for something you really want.

Don't be, don't ever be afraid to ask myself or President Screwem anything. We would love to have the CNAs do that.

Heidi and I will tell the other CNAs the good news, and we will start coming in tomorrow, OK President Screwem?

Oh yes, by all means please do, V.P. Howe and I would be delighted.

Great, it is settled then, it's a done deal, said Heidi, we will start this little operation tomorrow.

Splendid.

Splendid.

Do you have any more questions for Eric and Heidi, V.P. Howe?

Yes, just one. How do you two feel about the sign in the break room, petitioning FeudalCare employees to unionize.

I think it is disgusting.

1 agree, says Heidi, 1 don't want my hard-earned money going to no union dues.

That's right, Heidi, that money could go toward buying FeudalCare stock and make us a lot more money than any union can.

Eric is right, President Screwem and V. P. Howe. Don't get me wrong, unions were important a long time ago but there is no need for them today. Heidi, myself, and any FeudalCare employee can walk right in to your office any time if we have a problem or a complaint. We don't need a union. I think both of you would agree with President Screwem and myself, that you are paid excellent wages?

I agree, says Eric, I've looked around and our wages are competitive or exceed any nursing home in the area.

I am well compensated, agrees Heidi.

V.P. Howe and myself are very lucky to have two level headed young people such as yourselves heading our CNA staff.

Thank you, says Heidi.

Yes, and don't worry, President Screwem and V.P. Howe, Heidi and myself will see to it that no union brainwashes any of the CNAs.

Right, Eric, no unions are going to fool the CNAs at FeudalCare. Isn't that great, V.P. Howe?

Excellent, President Screwem, excellent.

Oh look, Fakewell and Roberson are here. Thank you so much for your input, Eric and Heidi, I speak for myself as well as President Screwem when I say I am delighted we had a chance to have our little talk and clear the air.

Me, too.

Me, too.

V.P. Howe and myself gained a great deal of respect for you two today. Thank you.

Thank you.

Heidi and Eric walk out the door and make sure they are far enough from the building so Screwem and Howe don't hear them. Then they burst out laughing.

Boy, do I need a beer after that shit, Heidi.

Likewise, wait till I tell that union organizer about this, Eric. He will die laughing.

Can you believe they swallowed that bullshit?

Of course, I can, Eric, there is a sucker born every minute as Barnum and Bailey used to say.

CHAPTER 11

Some Things You Just Don't Want to See

After the previous day's ordeal with Screwem and Howe, both Eric and Heidi were hoping for an uneventful evening. Their hope was in vain. A screaming and pounding noise was corning from Room 666. Eric and Heidi hoped they were hearing things and the noise would go away, no such luck.

We better check it out, Eric, it could be serious.

OK, I'II walk at a regular pace, instead of shuffling along like I usually do. Yea, I hate for the popcorn to get cold and to keep pausing *Teenage Mutant Ninja Turtles*, but we will be screwed if something is really wrong and we fail to check it out.

Heidi knocks on the door and she and Eric walk in. What you are about to find out is pretty gruesome, it is not for the faint of heart. If you have a weak or queasy stomach please close the book, set it down and go do something pleasant. Or, preferably, just skip this section and move on.

Wilma is lying stark naked, spread eagle on the bed. Her Moby Dick-like belly is protruding from the bed like Mt. Everest. Wrinkles and cellulite cover skin as far as the eye can see. She is holding a dixie cup.

Lamont is standing completely naked. His body is completely emaciated and his skin is every bit as wrinkled if not more so than Wilma. He is attempting to secure a plastic bag over his genitals with a rubber band.

Wilma, what are you doing? Heidi politely asks. Practicing.

Practicing what?

Practicing for sex. While Lamont is getting primed and prepped for the big event, I thought I better brush up on my skills. It has been years since I've done the old bump and grind.

How is screaming, yelling, and beating your head against the headboard practicing?

Every Adult Movie I've ever seen the woman always screams, yells, and the headboard bangs against the wall.

So why are you doing it?

If you are going to perform, you might as well emulate the best. And Adult Movies are the best?

They sure are.

What is the dixie cup for? Protection.

How is a dixie cup going to protect you?

I am going to use it as a diaphragm so I don't get pregnant.

Wilma, you are too old to get pregnant, and besides, a dixie cup can't prevent pregnancy.

The hell they can't. My family has used dixie cups as diaphragms for centuries, and they have prevented over 10,000 conceptions.

Whatever, Wilma, please get dressed and go back to your room, while I try to get this image out of my head so I won't be emotionally scarred for the rest of my life.

No, I want to have sex.

You can't.

Why not?

It is against FeudalCare policy. You two are not married and President Screwem and V.P. Howe would flip their lid.

To hell with Screwem and Howe, I want to make it with Lamont. Sorry, Wilma.

Man, you are worse than a 16-year-old girl's mom on prom night. I never get to have any fun.

Come on, Wilma.

Oh rats!

Eric tries to take the rise out of Lamont.

What are you doing, Lamont?

What do you think I am doing? I am getting ready to make it with Wilma. What is the plastic bag and rubber band get-up?

Protection, man, protection. I don't want to go having no children.

Lamont, Wilma is well past child bearing age, so pregnancy is not an issue. The plastic bag and rubber band isn't going to prevent anything.

You mean this here won't work?

No.

What do I need to do then?

Nothing, Lamont. Wilma can't get pregnant, but if she could, you would need a condom, which is specifically designed for a man, to prevent getting a woman pregnant.

I'll be damn, modern technology is unbelievable, what will they think of next?

Anyway, Lamont, you can't have sex with Wilma, you two are not married and it is against FeudalCare policy. Screwem and Howe would have a fit.

Ahhh shucks, you guys are a punch of kill-joys. You won't let a man have any fun.

Come on, Lamont, put your clothes back on and go to your own room. OK, damn, this sure turned out to be a lousy evening.

I know, Lamont, I know.

Lamont and Wilma mysteriously died that night. Extensive investigating, testing, and analysis was done following their deaths. It was discovered that at such an advanced age, sexually transmitted diseases can travel through the air, when two old people are naked in the same room together, even without physical contact.

Neither Lamont nor Wilma wanted to die that night. All they wanted to do was get laid. But, at least they went out striving to be the best they could be.

CHAPTER 12

What to Do with Daddy

It is with great sadness that Abdul and Ali, two devout Muslims, feel compelled to check their demented father Mohammed into a nursing home. Upon walking into the FeudalCare facility Abdul and Ali are immediately overcome with anger and sadness as they see a plaque with the saying: "Walk Humbly with God."

I thought America was supposed to be a secular country, Abdul.

I know, 1 was thinking the same thing, Ali. That is what I read in the constitution while I was studying for my U.S. citizenship test.

Didn't it say something about how church and state are supposed to be separate, Abdul?

Yes, it did, Ali! Next thing you know, they will be telling us we can't eat camel meat on Friday during lent, and putting "In God We Trust" on our currency.

Abdul, I am going into President Screwem and V.P. Howe's office tomorrow and tell those Great Satan's that I am deeply offended by that discriminatory plaque.

Now, now, Ali, calm yourself, I know the sign is very offensive to not only atheists and agnostics, but believers in other faiths and philosophies as well. Yes, Abdul, it is a slap in the face to Taoists, Buddhists, Muslims, and Hindus.

Seems like in America you can have freedom of religion as long as it is the Christian religion, Ali.

That is why I want to set those two infidels, Screwem and Howe, straight, Abdul.

I am in agreement with you, Ali, but with all the Anti-Muslim sentiment running rampant in America after 9/1 I it is best to keep our mouths shut.

I guess you are right, Abdul, we don't need the aggravation and Pop certainly doesn't need any more stress. If we piss Screwem and Howe off they may taint Pop's camel stew with pork and force him to drink a Budweiser,

Ali, so help me Allah, if they strip Pop's towel off his head and use it to clean the toilet or dry off some bed pans I will be furious.

I know, Abdul, not only are those towels expensive it would be very sacrilegious and irreverent to do that.

I really don't think we have to worry about that, Ali, surely Allah would destroy any infidel who attempts to use Pop's head towel as a cleaning or drying instrument.

Not only that, Abdul, if Pop's head is exposed to sunlight coming in from the window for too long, he could get heat stroke,

Abdul and Ali wheel their feeble father Mohammed into his room. With all the sorrow and anger they've experienced lately, Pop's declining health, not being able to care for him themselves, to the "Walk Humbly with God" plaque, they were pleasantly surprised that Pop got the bed by the window. That way, they could come every day, look out the window facing the sun, and pray with Pop to Allah. Ali immediately takes out Pop's Koran and places it on his night stand to counteract the falsehood and negative vibes spewing forth from his roommate Isaiah's Bible on his bedside table.

Mohammed, though he is feeble and demented, still has his lucid moments. He sees his roommate Isaiah's Bible and both brothers recognize that concerned look in his eye. They know exactly what he is thinking.

Don't worry, Pop, Abdul assures him, if FeudalCare runs low on toilet paper they will rip the pages out of Isaiah's Bible and not touch your Koran. Abdul and Ali unpack Pop's belongings, get him settled, and flip on his favorite TV show: *Allah Rules and God Drools.* This is not a local program by any stretch of the imagination, it comes right out of Tehran on the El Jazeer Network, Abdul and Ali are both multimillionaire oil sheiks. They had the program specially piped in at great expense for Pop to watch.

Abdul is a little apprehensive at first

Ali, I am afraid Pop's favorite program may offend some of the Christians in the nursing home, if they catch a glimpse of his TV.

You know what, Abdul, 1 was worried about the same thing a few minutes ago, but then I started thinking, those same residents did not care about offending us with the "Walk Humbly with God" plaque.

You are right, Ali.

So, I say fuckem if they can't take a joke, Abdul.

Abdul laughs deliriously and claps his hands at Ali's comment. Right on, bro! It is almost lunch time so they wheel Mohammed into the dining room, this being his first day and all. The brothers are relieved to see that another crisis has passed, Pop's favorite meal of camel meat and goats' milk has not been tampered with. In fact, it is quite tasty and the brothers are half tempted to ask the cook for the recipe. With all the anti-fossil fuel rhetoric and push for ethanol, the brothers are always looking for ways to safeguard and supplement their wealth. A restaurant specializing in camel meat and goats' milk would be a gold mine. Ali kinda likes the sound of Iranian Fried Camel, while Abdul is partial to Lawrence's Arabian Cuisine.

After lunch the brothers wheel Pop back into his room by the window facing Mecca. They got Pop seated in his Lazy Boy and Abdul reached for Pop's Koran. He and Ali were about to commence reading to Pop, when the phone at the front desk rang and interrupted them. At least the Charge Nurse answered with the proper dialogue.

FeudalCare, where we sterilize our bedpans and urinals once a week for your loved one's pleasure and comfort, may I help you?

Oh sorry, wrong number.

No problem, on behalf of FeudalCare have a great day. Thank you, goodbye.

Goodbye.

Anyway, the lights were on and Ali resumed reading. Abdul interrupted him with a frantic blood-curdling scream!

AHHHHH! Quick, get a doctor immediately! There is something drastically wrong with my father.

Nurse Tabitha angrily slams down her *Star Magazine* where she 1s reading an article about her favorite rock band Emesis and Saliva.

What is it?

I think my father is dead, he has been struck by lightning! Oh dear, let me get my stethoscope. I will be right back!

Nurse Tabitha takes Mohammed's vital signs and realizes Mohammed is not dead but in a motionless zombie state.

It is the damdest thing, he looks dead but he isn't. I've never seen anything like it, what in the world is going on?

Quickly she telephones Dr. McKenna.

Hello, this is Tabitha at FeudalCare Nursing Home. May I please speak to Dr. McKenna right away, it is an emergency.

I am sorry, ma'am, Dr. McKenna is on medical leave. I tried to warn him, but he just would not listen. It looks like the good doctor will finally have to, reluctantly, start chewing tobacco.

Oh my God, what happened?

He needs to have his other lung removed now.

Oh no, I wish he would have given up his cigarettes after the first lung removal, now it might be too late.

Dr. Oddadore is filling in for McKenna. I will send him right over. Dr. Oddadore walks across the street and examines Mohammed.

He is indeed alive but I have no idea what is wrong with him, I have never seen anything like this!

After 17 hours of tests, MRIs, CAT Scans etc. Mohammed is in the same condition and they still do not have any idea what is wrong with him. Exhausted, Ali, Abdul, and Dr. Oddadore wheel Mohammed outside for some fresh air. They sit down and relax for a few minutes. Suddenly another thunderstorm hits, accompanied by a huge bolt of lightning. Instantly Mohammed starts talking and moving around, right where he left off almost 24 hours ago. Needless to say, the three gentlemen are dumbfounded.

What in the world is going on here? says Dr. Oddadore. I don't think we will ever know, Abdul pipes in.

This is unbelievable, echoes Ali.

I have never seen anything like it in my thirty-five years of practicing medicine.

Ali is in favor of just dropping all conversation about the incident.

We could analyze this for 100 years and still not know what happened, let's not drive ourselves crazy trying to figure it out and just be grateful Pop is still alive.

Look, Ali, he is more than just alive, he is his old self again.

You are right, Abdul, he just used the restroom, showered, changed clothes and is reading the Koran, all by himself!

Praise Allah, Ali, Pop is cured, the lightning reconnected his brain signals, he is his old self again, good as new.

Jubilantly Ali and Abdul pack up Pop's belongings, check him out of the nursing home and head back to their estate, singing the praises and glory of Allah the whole way!

Before departing, Dad and the bros had a brief altercation with Nurse Dee Dee in the parking lot. Nurse Dee Dee was shouting at the top of her lungs, a song at them.

My God is better than your God, My God is better than yours,

My God's the Real God, cause he eats lamb not camel, My God is better than yours

Ali flipped her off and swore an Islamic Jihad.

CHAPTER 13

Not Your Grandpa's Pacemaker

Don't get me wrong, Screwem and Howe are two of the greatest, if not the greatest executives to ever walk the planet. There is simply no denying that. True they are a little behind the times when it comes to modern technology, but hey, after all, they are only human. It is not like they are Emperor Hirohito of World War II infamy, and gods in their own right. So what if it took them until 2003 to install indoor plumbing and electricity in the FeudalCare Nursing Horne. Hell, nobody is perfect. But even they would be surprised by this scenario.

Marvin woke up in the FeudalCare Nursing Horne alert and orientated one day after being transported from the hospital following heart surgery. He was in absolute despair. His wife Priscilla was there to support him.

Oh my gosh this is awful, I can't believe it. What, honey, what is it?

Oh, I knew I should have laid off the fast food and cigarettes all those years. Except for the time burglars broke into the house and I did not have a gun so I killed them by blowing second hand smoke into their face.

Marvin, it is OK, everything is going to be just fine, sweetie.

I should have exercised, too. All those years I said I was going to go to the gym and start working out, and I never did, it is really coming back to haunt me now.

Marvin, we've all made mistakes, but Dr. McKenna and Oddadore say you are going to be just fine, you've got a second chance.

And golf, oh no, I will never be able to golf again.

Why, of course you can golf again, Marvin, whatever gave you that idea?

How am I going to golf? It is not like they have electrical outlets and extension cords in the middle of the fairway and on the putting greens.

Why do you need electrical outlets and extension cords for golfing?

I will never be able to drive again either, or go in a car for that matter. I will have to spend my whole life inside the house in a JO-foot room.

Marvin, you are talking crazy, why are you saying all this stuff? You are not making any sense.

Where am I plugged in now, Priscilla? Do I have a long enough chord to walk to the bathroom?

What plug, what chord? You don't have any plug or chord, you can walk anywhere you want to.

If I don't have a chord, that means I must be dead and you must be dead, too, and we are talking up in heaven, or maybe down in hell?

Marvin, you are alive and getting better, I am here for you, what is going on?

So, I did not need the pacemaker after all?

You have the pacemaker inside you right now, the doctors say it is working fine, you can go home tomorrow.

I have to admit I feel good, but how can I have a pacemaker without an electrical cord and outlet? There is no way, that's too good to be true.

You do not need an electrical cord and outlet for a pacemaker, whatever gave you that idea?

When I was a little boy, my grandpa had a pacemaker. It was run by electricity and it had to be plugged into an electrical outlet and it only had a 10-foot chord. He had to spend the rest of his life in that small 10-foot room, and could only walk the length of the chord. The house had to be equipped with a back-up generator in case there was a power failure. It was awful, he could not go anywhere in a car, he could not go for a walk, nothing, unless it was in that damn 10-foot room. The pacemaker was huge, too. It weighed about 20 pounds and hung around his neck, he had a hole drilled in his back for the wires to come out. The pacemaker almost strangled him. He hated it. That does sound awful, Marvin, I can see now why you were frightened.

I'll say, one time a dog got in his room and tried to attack him, he started running and came unplugged. He sputtered and sparked around on the ground like a defective firecracker. It damn near killed him.

What happened?

Scared the shit out of that stray dog, he charged out Grandpa's room and out of the house faster than a snowball melts in hell.

No, I mean what happened to your Grandpa?

Oh, Dad saw him and plugged him back in. Another time he almost got electrocuted taking a shower.

How awful.

Dad tried to make a chord that could plug into the cigarette lighter in the car, so Grandpa could drive and go on trips with us. He tried everything to help Grandpa, a gasoline pacemaker, that exploded and damn near blew Grandpa to the moon. You name it, Dad tried it, but it was all to no avail. Grandpa died a dejected man.

Well, honey, now they have battery-operated pacemakers. You can walk, drive, golf, do anything you want to do, with no limitations.

That is wonderful, Priscilla, I feel luckier than a fat man in a bowl of chocolate syrup. What happens when the battery runs dead, though?

Well, that is a little tricky, Marvin, you do need to stick your finger in an electrical outlet. Be careful your hair is not wet, or you will look like Don King.

Oh, Priscilla, that is terrible.

I'm just kidding, Marvin. They have special instruments that check the battery once every six months. It is able to recharge it if need be, and it is perfectly safe and painless, you won't feel a thing.

Wow, Priscilla, Grandpa would sure be impressed, and envious of me.

CHAPTER 14

Just Shoot Me

Poor Phil, age 95, was in real bad physical shape. To say his health was failing is to put it mildly. He had chronic heart disease, a stroke, peripheral vascular disease and was on oxygen. CNA Rita, not the brightest bulb on the branch, i.e. A Dip-Shit Aide, upon seeing Phil, commented, you don't look too good today, Phil.

I am 95 years old and on life supports. I am not supposed to look good, goddamn it!

I am sorry, Phil. When the triage nurse checked you in, did she have you sign a DNR?

What's that?

In the event you stop breathing, it states that you do not want to be brought back to life.

No, but it is a damn good idea, hell I'd just as soon they take me out back and shoot me right now. Where the hell did I set my teeth, goddamn it?

They are right here.

Thank you.

No problem, Phil.

Shit, I am out of Life-Savers again.

Phil, you have your Life-Savers right in your hand. Damn, I wonder how they got there?

Anyway, I can take care of the DNR for you. You are of sound mind aren't you?

Yes, I am of sound mind. It is my body that is fucked up, not my mind. OK, OK, don't get upset, Phil.

Shit, I am not upset.

Your doctor wants you to wear Ted Hose. What's that?

They are tightly wound fish net stockings that are supposed to improve circulation in your legs.

Oh Christ, I ain't gonna wear those sissy things. Listen, there ain't nothin' gonna help my circulation.

Phil, if you don't wear the Ted Hose, a blood clot could form in your leg and give you another stroke. This time you might not be so lucky, and it could kill you.

You people are fucking nuts. I am 95 years old and have lived a great life. My health sucks. There ain't nothin' that's gonna change that. My time is up, it is time for me to go. I should be so lucky as to bite the dust right now.

Oh, don't talk that way, Phil.

Ahhh you people are a pain in the ass, I am disgusted with every last one of ya.

Phil, I am going to give you a specimen cup and a hat. What for?

Dr. McKenna is back from his lungectomy, and wants to run some urine and stool tests. When you have a BM, you need to mark it on this BM sheet.

Ahhh, for Christ's sake that damn Doctor needs to mind his own goddamn business and worry about himself, and leave me the hell alone to die.

Please cooperate with me, Phil.

I'm a grown man, I ain't gonna shit and piss in a cup, and mark it down on a sheet of paper for no Doctor to analyze. I'm gonna die within six months anyway, ain't no blood, shit, or piss test gonna change that. Please let me die with peace and dignity.

If you feel that way, Phil, why did you come to FeudalCare in the first place.

It's that dad-blasted son of mine. He wants to keep me alive at all costs regardless of my quality of life. I am surprised he hasn't petitioned Congress to pass an Eternal Life Amendment.

I see, Phil.

It is not just my family, it is our whole society. We have this paranoia about death. That it is somehow bad, wrong and evil and that it should be avoided at all costs.

I never thought about that, Phil.

Well, I am here to tell you that it is not. It is OK to die. There is nothing wrong with dying.

What would you like me to do, Phil?

Come in here and shoot the shit with me every once in a while. Tell me a funny joke, and help me walk around a little bit with this here support belt.

It is called a gait belt.

OK, then do that.

I promise I will, Phil. My name is Rita and I am the Aide that services Broadway, that is the hall you are on.

Hell, I always wanted to be on Broadway, but to sing and dance, not die. Chuckle from Rita.

Rita?

Yea, Phil?

This here ankle bracelet is killing me. It is way too tight, my ankle is all red and swollen, and it is cutting a hole into my leg.

Oh, that is so you don't wander off the premises, if you open the door to exit the building, it sets off an alarm.

Oh yea, in my condition, like I am really gonna go out and run a marathon and stay out all night getting drunk. Why don't you give me a handful of condoms while you're at it, like I am gonna use them, too.

I'll tell you what, Phil, I'm not supposed to do this and I can get in big trouble from President Screwem and Vice President Howe, so you have to swear you won't tell a soul.

I am very good at swearing in case you haven't noticed, Rita. I noticed, Phil.

Seriously, though, Rita, I promise I won't tell a soul, not a word from me, Old Phil's lips are sealed. I ain't no snitch. What have ya got in mind, Rita?

I'm gonna cut off your wanderguard. My what?

Your wanderguard, that bracelet you have around your ankle. Oh God, Rita, that would be great.

Now keep your sweat pants low to cover your ankle, so no one notices.

Especially Nurse Dee Dee.

Oh, I heard she is a real bitch. You bet she is.

Your secret is safe with me, Rita, mum's the word, I feel so much better already. Can you get me some scotch tape, Rita?

Why, are you making a scrap book or something?

Hell no, I want to fix this skin tear on my arm and stop it from bleeding. Oh, Phil, you can't fix a skin tear with scotch tape.

Well, what can I do then?

I will tell the Nurse to put a sterile pad on it.

Of course, I am sterile, Rita. I ain't gonna go fathering any more children at my age, especially on account of how sick I am.

No, Phil, sterile means clean.

Oh, boy do I feel like a horse's ass. Don't, Phil, you are a cool guy.

Thanks, Rita.

No problem, Phil.

Rita walks out of the room, but turns back because she thinks Phil is gasping for air. Upon reentering the room, Rita notices that Phil is in respiratory distress. He is fishing breathing, you know, where your lips pucker in and out. Against Phil's wishes, because the DNR did not get signed, Rita is forced to call Lifeline. Lifeline came and put Phil on the bus to the amusement park. Phil's condition is grave, too dangerous for either intensive care light, or even semi-intensive care.

His only chance for survival is to be rushed up to extra industrial strength super intensive care.

Dr. Oddadore and McKenna did everything they could to save Phil, but it was to no avail. Phil's time was up. He checked out and was headed up to that 24 hours a day, 7 days a week party in the sky.

Rita accidently marked down that Phil had a BM before he died, but in reality, he didn't. Fortunately, Rita's mom was a public notary. She was able to get a hold of her mom and have the mistaken BM on Phil's sheet notarized. With a sigh of relief Rita avoid the wrath of Nurse Dee Dee, and was able to keep her valuable CNA License.

Rita never forgot the lessons she learned on a cold, frigid December day from her mentor Phil.

CHAPTER 15

Blow Me Up

When you think of a resident in a nursing home, your mind conjures up images of old, feeble and senile people to name but a few. Nathan did not fit that description by any stretch of the imagination. He was 53 years old, very distinguished looking, graying ever so slightly at the temples, tall, and with an athletic physique. As a matter of fact, Nathan frequently entered l OK races and lifted weights. To be honest with you, Nathan looked like the picture of health. So you can imagine the shock on Nurse Tilly's face when she entered Nathan's room.

Hello, my name is Nurse Tilly, I will be your Nur, Oh my!

An equally confused Nathan responded with, Excuse me? Did I do something wrong? I realize I am no Matthew McConaughey, but I don't look that bad, do I?

No, No, not at all.

Then what is the problem?

Well, working in a nursing home, I am used to seeing old, sickly people, I was not expecting someone so young and ahhh...

Handsome as myself.

Well, yes, responded a blushing Nurse Tilly.

Why, thank you, I will take that as a compliment then.

You should, by the way, what are you in the nursing home for? Oh, I had a trim.

You are in the nursing home because you had a haircut?

No.

I don't follow what you mean by a trim then.

I had an enlarged prostate, that was obstructing my urine flow. So, I had a prostatectomy.

Oh, I see, that is why you call it a trim. Your prostate was trimmed. Yes.

Cute.

Thank you.

So, are you here to recuperate from the surgery?

Well, sort of, you see, when I was in the hospital, I suffered from a complication.

Oh, gee I am sorry to hear that, is it serious?

No, just kind of embarrassing and aggravating. It is more of a nuisance than anything else.

What happened?

I needed a catheter following my surgery. Turns out, a student Nurse inserted that catheter, and when she inflated the balloon to keep the catheter in place in my bladder, she made a mistake.

What kind of a mistake?

She inflated it with helium, instead of water. Oh my gosh, that is awful.

After she inflated it, she left the room and closed the door. Then all of a sudden, the helium must have expanded or something. I floated up in the air and banged my head on the ceiling. It is a damn good think the ceiling window was closed, otherwise I might have bumped into a 747 or rocket in the sky.

You poor thing, then what happened?

I was up in the air yelling for two hours, but no one heard me. What did you do?

I destroyed a couple of cobwebs, and tied the legs of some spiders together.

No, I mean how did you finally get down?

Housekeeping finally opened the door and saw me. Didn't your roommate help you?

No.

Why not?

He was so busy lying on his back and using his leg cast to pound nails into the wall, to even hear or notice me.

That does not sound good.

No, it wasn't. It wasn't very smart on his part either.

I should say not. Sounds like you had a hell of an ordeal. I'll say, and it gets even better, or worse I should say.

Then what happened?

The janitor had to climb up on a step ladder to reach me. He stuck a hypodermic needle up my ass to puncture the balloon.

That sounds dangerous, Nathan.

It was, the balloon popped and I fell to the floor like a ton of bricks. I fractured my tail bone, and here I am to rehabilitate for a month or so, maybe longer.

What a weird experience, Nathan, I have never heard anything like that. I'll say, I was considering a penile implant, but after that catheter experience, I am afraid that damn hospital will blow up my penis and testicles, and they will explode.

You have really had bad luck, Nathan.

Actually, I have been pretty lucky up until now. My brother and sister, they've really faced disappointment in their life.

How?

Ever since I can remember they both wanted more than anything in the world to be professional models. They always had the latest fashion in clothing and hairstyles, and always got just the right amount of sun. They exercised regularly, and ate healthy foods. One day, they thought they finally had their big break. They got a call from *Vogue*, but it was not the modeling magazine *Vogue*, it was a company that prints pamphlets about genital and sexually transmitted diseases. They wound up getting their genitals covered with make-up, to make it look like they had all kinds of diseases and stuff, it was awful. They took the job and wound up having their diseased-looking genitals photographed. For the longest time, they were so embarrassed and disappointed.

Why didn't they turn the job down?

They couldn't. Why not?

They needed the money, they were deeply in debt with all the money they laid out to go to modeling school.

That must have been a very difficult time for them, Nathan. Those aren't exactly the type of photographs you want to go running home to show Mom, Dad, and friends.

You are right, Tilly, it is not like you can go bragging to Mom about a picture of your genitals with gonorrhea or syphilis,

Did they continue pursuing their modeling careers after that?

No, they both went on to be social workers and just recently celebrated their 25th year on the job, Marvelous.

Yea, they both adjusted very well and are happy with the way their life turned out.

Nathan's prostate and sexual prowess made a complete recovery. After he was released from the nursing home he started dating Nurse Tilly. A year after that they were married. Tilly just has to be careful not to hum the lyrics to "Up, Up, and Away in My Beautiful Balloon" when Nathan is around.

CHAPTER 16

Let's Call It a Wrap

It is my fondest wish and sincerest desire that you enjoyed your journey into the world of FeudalCare. It is really quite a place isn't it? I am sure you got to know most of the characters so well, that they were like members of your own family. I thought about how cruel and unfair it would be not to let you know what happened to them.

Nurse Dee Dee left FeudalCare and became a nun. Since the death of Mother Teresa there has been a huge void in the humanitarian and missionary work area. Nurse Dee Dee, being a selfless individual, felt a calling from God to fill the gap. The Catholic Church did have to make a slight concession, however. Weekly she receives a shipment of fast food, vodka, cigarettes, donuts, candy, potato chips, cookies, Coca Cola and men. She is also allowed to play poker on line in her tent. Hey, come on, Nurse Dee Dee does have a life you know! And, she still diets regularly.

President Screwem and Vice President Howe tragically had their lives cut short when they were both bitten by a resident with rabies. Since FeudalCare knew they only had a week to live they offered them free food, lodging and care for the remainder of their time here on earth. Both declined.

President Screwem was heard to say, Hell no, 1 would not be caught dead living in a dump like that.

They were cremated together and their ashes where permanently enshrined in the ashtray out in the smoke hut. They were both inducted into the FeudalCare Hall of Fame and their scrubs hang from the ceiling in the FeudalCare Corporate Office.

Nurse Tilly and Nathan are still married, and making a ton of dough in the pornography industry.

Nurse Tabitha is in medical school. She felt that it was time Doctors stopped practicing medicine and start doing it right. She wants to start the trend.

Nurse Gretel now works for the Psychic Hotline.

Eric and Heidi opened up a funeral parlor when they realized the quantity of dead people FeudalCare pumped out each year.

Allah continues to bless Abdul and Ali. Today they own a chain of Iranian Fried Camel Restaurants. Mohammed is lucid enough to wipe down tables and pass out camel sauce at one of the local restaurants.

Diane Smells was able to get a full-time gig lecturing on" How to get the most for the least from your employees."

No one even knew Kitty died because the obituary was hidden.

Raymond sells lie detectors, is still driving his wife Samantha crazy, and trying to come to grips with his smoking fetish.

Ruthy is a counselor at an insane asylum. Gee, 1 wonder what prompted her to take a job in that line of work?

Jacintha is still working at FeudalCare as a CNA.

Janitor Norby and Floor Washer Cliffy are in jail. They saw the movie *Home Alone* and emulated Harry and Marv.

Janey and Rachel never did get their dream job at the prison. The current Republican Administration really cranked up the implementation and utilization of the death penalty. Prisons are practically empty. Realizing what a huge need there is for properly trained (unbrainwashed) CNAs, with a huge government grant they started their own CNA Training School. There motto is "We Do CNAs Right."

Roberta and Jimmy both work in the pharmaceutical industry for Defy Inc. and are trying to perfect and patent bagless catheters and colostomy bags. 1 guess they would just be called colostomy then.

Dr. McKenna lost his struggle to be the first man in history to live with both lungs removed and still chew tobacco.

Dr. Oddadore is a strange Doctor, he continues to look for love in all the wrong places.

Marvin and Priscilla work for the U.S. Army. Priscilla pushes Marvin around in a wheel barrel so Marvin's pacemaker can detect land mines.

Rita was deeply moved by her experience taking care of Phil before his death, and as a result went on to pursue a career as a Geriatric Psychologist, and she works at the circus part time on weekends as the bearded lady to help make ends meet.

Andy's effort at implementing athletic competition at FeudalCare did not go unnoticed. He was offered a job as a trainer for the Special Olympics. He is about to come off suspension for yelling at the top of his lungs over the P.A. System to the hearing-impaired team, get out of bed, what are you deaf or something?

1 want to apologize for not knowing what happened to the other minor cast and characters, they were simply acquaintances, 1 lost touch with them.

Bye bye, you all, take care not to have a Feudal day!!

THINGS GO WRONG
The Wander Daze Part 2

CHAPTER 1
Nurse Dee Dee is Back in Town

The Maestro strikes up the orchestra:
Nurse Dee Dee is back in town FeudalCare is going crazy,
they can't believe how lucky they are they thought they lost
their princess forever, Nurse Dee Dee is back in town.

CNA Jacintha is fantasizing. Since the untimely demise of President Screwem and Vice President Howe, FeudalCare has been in a downward spiral. In what seemed like a split second, FeudalCare went from being the premiere nursing home on the planet, to the depths of despair. The chief reason being, the nursing staff was no longer being held under the thumb of an all-knowing omnipotent ruler.

Things had really gotten out of hand, employee meals were being provided free of charge, unlike the President Screwem special, "buy one get the second for double." Fifteen-minute breaks were now being allowed every shift, and the worse rub of all, employees were enjoying coming to work. For God sake there was not even a bolshitvabok (employee handbook) on the premises. Nursing homes thrive on making staff members feel that no matter what they do, it just is not good enough. That feeling at FeudalCare was slipping away. Rumor has it some were even singing as they went about their daily tasks. CNA didn't even mind going into residents' rooms with c-diff. (stool infection)

The penal system was still vintage healthcare. If it is trivial make it important, if it is important make it trivial, the equivalent of the death penalty for jaywalking. However, laxness had definitely set in at FeudalCare. Employees were being treated as adults and did not have to sign off that they completed their tasks.

The dot system, where if you have the dot by your name you have to work another shift if someone does not show up, was not used once since Screwem and Howe departed for that great big nursing home in the sky. Consequently, no one was being imprisoned for dot fraud (erasing the dot next to your name and putting it by someone else). Prisons contained only HIPPA violators, those who upwardly forged the percentage of a meal a resident ate, and those guilty of urine fraud. Falsifying how much a resident peed during a given shift. The only dot system being used is the dot to dot system for graphing vital signs of hospice patients to save their life.

FeudalCare was not facing a crisis like nuclear war, a terrorist attack, running out of q-tips, or someone putting flyers in car windshields. The bottom line was still intact, granted it was not at the extraordinary clip that it was under Screwem's reign, but Screwem was a godlike figure whose results could never be duplicated. Too even hint at it would be absurd.

First shit, I mean first shift nurses still hated life, however there was an intangible source of agitation in management no one could directly put their finger on. Subconsciously though, I think every member of The Board of Directors knew what it was. But, like an autographed soiled diaper hidden on E-bay, it needed to be flushed out. Genius sometimes comes from the most unexpected places, like a bag of trash down the laundry shoot!!

CNA Jacintha was by no means old, but she sure acted like it. She was definitely not on top of her game. On more than one occasion she was written up for writing "not much of anything" on a residents' plan of care. Any time she was asked why a resident did a certain behavior her pat answer was "because they are old."

When Jacintha placed her suggestion in the employee comment box, the last thing on her mind, (what little mind she has) was the profit and loss statement of FeudalCare. She just wanted her old Christian buddy Dee Dee back, to take smoke breaks with, and talk about how godly they are. Little did she realize her suggestion would bring about something as improbable as germs escaping from a hazard bag in an isolation room, or the spouse of an Alzheimer's' resident having extramarital relations, her suggestion fueled in a whole new era in FeudalCare history, the Screwem and Howe era was officially over, it was a new millennium, the President Dee Dee era!

"Hello operator, this is Dick Vajeanya I am on the Board of Directors at FeudalCare Nursing Home, I'd like to place an international call to Calcutta, India."

"Who would you like to speak to sir?"

"A Sister Dee Dee Kuntz she is at the local missionary base in Calcutta."

"Very good sir I am connecting you right now have a Jesus filled Day."

"Is that anything like a Jelly filled doughnut?"

"Excuse me sir?"

"Oh, never mind."

"Hello, Sister Dee Dee?" "Speaking"

"This is Dick Vajeanya."

""Who"

"Dick Vajeanya I'm on the Board of Directors at FeudalCare Nursing Home."

"Oh Wow! FeudalCare, God I miss that place. Don't get me wrong, I love doing the Lords work here.in India, combining my medical expertise and spirituality, to keep these scumbags alive, so I can save their souls and send them to heaven. But, I will always have a soft spot in my soul for FeudalCare."

"I was hoping you'd say that Sister Dee Dee." "Why is that, what do you mean?"

"Well, FeudalCare has been in dire straits since President Screwem and Vice President Howe died. I can't begin to tell you what a pain in the <u>geri-ass-trics</u> it has been."

"Oh my God, when did that happen?" "Oh, about six months ago, Sister Dee Dee

"Jesus (excuse me Lord) I didn't know, I've been so busy doing The Lords work here in India, I have not kept up on any news from the states."

"I know Sister Dee Dee, I know."

"Even if I were not so busy saving the souls of all these despicable heathens, The Calcutta Times is so dreadful, I would not have known anyway. What happened, how did they die?"

"This resident, a real asshole had rabies, bit them while they were reprimanding a CNA for using too many wet wipes and lotion."

"Using wet wipes and lotion on those wrinkly ass old people cost a fortune Dick! Those old sacks of shit need to lie there and suffer. Jesus loves suffering and penance, it's good for them."

The CNA in question said, "I used all those wet wipes and lotion because the resident said her buttock was sore."

"I don't give a shit if her ass- burns, buy some aspirin, leave our ointment and wet wipes alone!

"Good point Sister Dee Dee we need to put a halt to this nonsense, and pronto!!"

"It is too bad that loser didn't bite a CNA instead of our beloved Screwem and Howe, Dick, it is a damn shame!"

"Indeed Dee Dee, CNA.'s are a dime a dozen but executives like Screwem and Howe are special, they come around once a lifetime, if that."

"That really sucks Dick."

"That is not the worst of it Sister Dee Dee." "You mean there is more."

"Yes, Sister Dee Dee I am afraid so. Unfortunately, the euthanasia nurse cremated the wrong bodies."

"Oh no, Dick, that is terrible!"

"Yes, turns out she walked into the wrong room. I think she was oxygen deprived from smoking thru a surgical mask, some germ fetish or something. Anyway, she saw a decrepit old man and woman with their feeding tubes and oxygen off. She thought they were Dewey and Anne, and cremated the body's right outside the nursing home."

"Why were there feeding tubes and oxygen off Dick?" "They had to be roto- rootered out. Seems their kids went to Old Country Buffet and brought back some leftovers for mom and dad. They were always bitching about the food. No matter what was on the menu, they always wanted the substitute. The kids, tried to stuff the chicken and mash potatoes through the feeding tube."

"Oh no Dick, that is worse than a CNA cutting a diabetic toe nails, or a student nurse giving a doctors consult."

"I know Sister Dee Dee, can you believe they tried shoving 360 cc of chicken and mash potatoes down those feeding tubes."

"Damn it Dick, I hate that God Damn metric system. If ounces and pounds were good enough for Jesus Christ, they are good enough for me too. What is 360cc in English?"

"Oh, I am sorry Dee Dee, my bad, 360cc is 12 ounces." "Thank you, sir, that is much better."

"You are not going to believe this Dee Dee but it gets worse still."

"How could it sir?"

"We were having a cookout and the old folk's kids did not order desert at Old Country Buffet, so they stopped outside to toast a few marshmallows, over the bonfire."

"Good God Dick!"

"Yes Dee Dee, unbeknownst to the kids, they were roasting marshmallows over the flames of their smoldering parents."

"Heavens to Betsy, what did the kids say when they found out, Dick?"

"Nothing, they never found out, we covered it up Sister Dee Dee."

"How the hell did you do that Dick?"

"It was not a problem at all Sister Dee Dee. I don't get off on being honest and helping people, especially ones that can no longer put any money in my pocket."

"That is right Dick, because you are a good Christian." "Why thank you Sister Dee Dee, I am a good Christian!" "My pleasure Dick, you certainly are a good Christian, the second best."

"We got the kids snowed on grain alcohol and haldol. They were so wasted, when we told them their mom and dad passed away in their sleep, they bought it Sister Dee Dee." "Thank goodness Dick."

"Sister Dee Dee, they were so stoned, they did not even notice the dead bodies were not their parents, but rather the bodies of Screwem and Howe. Then the euthanasia nurse immediately cremated Screwem and Howe's bodies, and enshrined their ashes in the employee smoke hut."

"You are a genius Mr. Vajeanya."

"Why thank you Sister Dee Dee, you are way to kind, I was just lucky, actually, I almost blew it."

"I am sure you are just being modest Dick, I can't imagine you making a mistake."

"Well Sister Dee Dee, I almost forgot to have a CNA shave the hair on Anne Howe's upper lip. That would have been a dead giveaway."

"Well the important thing is you did remember to shave her, Dick. First thing I did every morning was make sure the C.N.A's. shaved all my residents. If I was running the show none of this nonsense would happen. I'd put a stop to these mistakes immediately."

"Funny you should mention that Sister Dee Dee because that is exactly why I am calling."

"What, are you serious?"

"Yes, Sister Dee Dee I am dead serious (no disrespect to the late Dewey Screwem and Anne Howe) I would love to have you back at FeudalCare, and this time you would not be just a floor nurse, you would be running the whole show!"

"Really, oh gosh, I would love to be in charge of the whole place. I would be like an old clinical instructor I had. I would demand employees hurry up, stamping my feet hut 2, 3, 4, hut 2, 3, 4."

"Sister Dee Dee this place really lacks a domineering zealot since Screwem and Howe died. We could really use you too carry on their legacy."

"Oh my, I'm so flattered, I am speechless, I don't know what to say. Since Dewey and Anne can't be cloned, I am FeudalCare's only chance for survival. There is no room for error in this profession, I NEVER make a mistake, unlike some dumb asses who inject the wrong insulin."

"Say yes Dee Dee and make me the happiest man in the world. You are ideal for the job Dee Dee and you yourself even said you are FeudalCares only chance for survival."

"What about the smoking ban, I'd hate to have to run out to the smoke hut every time I want to light up."

"I will wave it for you Dee Dee. You can smoke anywhere on the premises."

"Things are really bad, aren't they Dick?"

"I'll say Sr. Dee Dee, the President we have now does not even strip search the staff for contraband."

"What a wuss"

"Sister Dee Dee this new guy is a real light weight. He lacks the witch hunt mentality. He fails to realize how important it is for an authority figure to nail someone's ass to the wall for no rhyme or reason."

"That is terrible Dick, just terrible."

"It is awful Dee Dee, CNA's are being paid a living wage, the union has a foot in the door, and I actually heard a CNA humming in the hallway."

"Boy things have sure changed Dick I remember how Screwem and Howe had every CNA filled with hate and self loathing."

"Sister Dee Dee, CNA's definitely lack the fear of God Dewey Screwem and Anne Howe instilled. Get a load of this Dee Dee we even have some nurses now who don't smoke."

"What! And they call themselves nurses! That is too bad, so sad Dick"

"Profits are still OK Dee Dee but FeudalCare has definitely lost that Corporate America feeling."

"What upsets me the most Dick is the idea of a CNA being paid a living wage. That is atrocious, I won't stand for it! That money needs to be earmarked for legal fees, to prevent C. N. A.'s from getting their share of the pie!"

"Precisely Dee Dee we are the head honcho's, if you fail to make a CNA' feel crazy and evil for fighting back when we abuse them, you are finished in this business. Dee Dee I really like what you said about spending money on defense attorneys and legal fees. Battling employees really builds the moral of our top executives and fires up major shareholders." "Thank you, Dick, I believe that with every fiber of my being. I accept your offer to become the next President of Feuda!Care."

"You mean you will take the job Dee Dee?"

"Do old people like to drive 10 mph with their left hand turn signal on? Of course, I will take the job."

"Marvelous Sister, I mean President Dee Dee. How soon can you get here?"

"Quicker than you can see a liver spot on a 98-year-old man, I will email the head of the mission, that I am resigning immediately and I will be catching the first plane out of here."

"You don't have to give a two-week notice?"

"Screw the mission. I am out of here. I am President Dee Dee now."

"Wonderful, I will see you as soon as you get into town." "OK Dick, by the way, can I borrow a tank of gas and some money from petty cash for smokes. I will be short on money till I get my first FeudalCare check."

"Sure, Dee Dee no problem, I can give you an advance." "Great, thank you Mr. Vajeanya. See you when I get in." "Good Bye President Dee Dee."

"Good-Bye Dick"

CHAPTER 2

Restoring Fiscal Responsibility

Two days later Nurse Dee is back in town to hammer out her contract and finalize the deal to be FeudalCare's next President. For a moment she is awestruck as she heads toward the building thinking of the tremendous shoes she has to fill following President Dwight "Dewey" Screwem.

President Dee Dee has had tremendous success quitting smoking she has done it literally thousands of times. With tension in the atmosphere and a knot in her stomach this is not going to be one of those times. The big moment has her as aroused as an 80-year-old man wanting to jump the bones of a young CNA It looks like she is literally starving for air! Like one of her diets, quitting will have to wait. She lights up a cigarette to calm her nerves and thinks to herself, this is an excellent opportunity to make sure Vajeanya is not just blowing smoke up my ass, and that he intends to follow through on his promise to lift the smoking ban. Good sign, upon greeting Vajeanya in the Board of Directors lounge, with cigarette in hand, Vajeanya offers her an ashtray.

"Shit, Mr. Vajeanya, I forgot to put on my cheese stick patch to curb my hunger. I'm starved. Do you have any donuts and hot chocolate?"

Vajeanya pushes a button and secretary Buffy responds, "May I help you Mr. Vajeanya?"

Suddenly there is a knock on the window and both Dee Dee and Vajeanya tum around but no one is there, jubilantly Dee Dee jumps up.

"It is the ghost of Screwem and Howe. They are signaling they're in favor of me becoming FeudalCare's next president and the Lord gives it his blessing. Oh, I am so excited, this is just wonderful!"

Vajeanya clears his throat and says, "yes I quite agree Dee Dee" Buffy looks at them both acting like raving lunatics, but says nothing, "May I help you Mr. Vajeanya?"

"Yes Buffy, my apology for the delay."

"That is quite alright sir says Buffy," as she rolls her eyes. "Thank you, Buffy."

"You are welcome sir."

Vajeanya is only 60 years old, not quite old enough yet for Alzheimer's disease, but at times he does have temporary memory lapses, which is a good indication he has some-timers disease.

"Yes, now, where were we?"

"My doughnuts Dick, I am famished."

"Oh, ok, now I remember, Buffy could you run across the street and buy a dozen donuts and a large hot chocolate?"

"I don't think a dozen donuts will be enough Dick, it was an extremely long plane trip, I am famished."

"Make it two dozen then." "That's better, thank you Dick."

Not more than two minutes after Buffy walks out the door, Dick shows another symptom of his some-timers. He remembers he forgot to tell Buffy to get him a large coffee with cream and sugar. Dick removes his rotary cell phone from the holster on his waist. There must be something in the water that upper management drinks at FeudalCare. If you recall, the late Screwem and Howe, had an affinity for Mr. Ed as well. Vajeanya places the pencil in his mouth and begins to dial Buffy's number.

"Oh, hi Buffy, listen, could you get me a large black coffee with cream and sugar, in addition to the two dozen donuts and hot chocolate?"

"Sure Mr. Vajeanya, but you did not give me any money for that."

"Oh for God sake Buffy, it is only a dollar I will pay you when you get back."

Normally Buffy would not care about a dollar, but since Dick Vajeanya throws nickels around like they are man whole covers, she thought she better press the issue. Moments later Buffy returns with the nectar of life, and President Dee Dee immediately rips open the box and begins to chow down, stuffing her face like a starving pit bull.

"God, this is good", mutters President Dee Dee, her mouth stuffed with donuts, and hot chocolate smeared all over her face, making an absolute pig of herself1 In between bites she mutters," I can't wait for lunch."

Finally, after wolfing down two dozen donuts President Dee Dee is ready for Dick Vajeanya to talk.

"Dee Dee, it is so good to have you back, FeudalCare has so many problems, I don't know where to start."

President Dee Dee lets out a huge belch, and comments on how much better she feels, now.

"Just start at the top of your head Dick, and take one issue at a time."

"Well Dee Dee, the first order of business and obviously the most important is wages. After Screwem and Howe died, some Phil Donahue limp wrested weenie type, took over and gave CNA's a raise. He mentioned some liberal bullshit about cost of living indexes, how CNA's wages had not been adjusted for inflation since the Kennedy Administration and a bunch of other nonsense. He gave everyone a $2 an hour pay raise. He is one of those 1960' hippie freaks who acts like authority sucks. There went Mrs. Vajeanya's yacht that I was going to buy her for her birthday. It has been terrible Dee Dee, I've had to sell one of my Rolls Royce's, I've only bought 2 new Armani suits this year, and I'm smoking Swisher Sweet cigars! For 12 years when Screwem and Howe were running "the show" it was nothing but imported Cuban cigars. Now, I'm smoking fucking Swisher Sweets! Can you imagine a man of my caliber and stature smoking Swisher Sweets? This nonsense has to stop. And, that is only the tip of the iceberg of the devastating injustices I've had to endure, since Mr. Liberal started his living wage Bullshit!"

"Calm down Dick you're going to give yourself a stroke." 'know Dee Dee you're right, I'm sorry, it's just so damn aggravating."

"I empathize with you Dick, I will straighten things out, I promise. The money spent on giving CNA's a living wage, could go toward surgery to fix these ugly pock marks in my face. As it stands now, I am going to have to use a green- beret knife and silly putty to perform my own plastic surgery." "Oh, come on President Dee Dee you are beautiful!" "Aww Dick", a blushing President Dee Dee responds, "you are too kind."

"Anyway Dee Dee, any suggestions about how to get these wages back under control?"

"Yes, Dick I have just the plan to restore fiscal responsibility.

"OHHHH, President Dee Dee fiscal responsibility, sounds so "REPUBLICANISH!"

"Yes, I know. You like it?" "Like it Dee Dee, I love it!"

"Good, then what I propose is that we cut wages very secretively and in a discreet manner, so as not to upset the ACLU, worker's rights groups, or any other of those "pinko commie" organizations. Thank God CNA's are stupid, they lack any insight whatsoever, they don't analyze anything because they are too busy fighting amongst themselves. Therefore, we can stick it up their ass without them even knowing it."

"Brilliant Dee Dee, brilliant, but whatever you do, don't bring this up when you are talking to any of the CNA's, if they ever got wind of how we are screwing them, all hell would break lose."

"You don't have to worry about me blabbing Dick, mum is the word. But, even if I did mention it, not only would they be too ignorant to understand, they would be too apathetic to do anything about it."

"Well, you are right Dee Dee, but let's ere on the side of caution and play it safe anyway."

"You got it Dick you have nothing to worry about. Why just as I was walking in a heard a C.N.A spewing forth some of the brainwashed propaganda we feed them." "She said, I always keep myself busy, if any one needs help, I jump right in. I don't go and hide like other CNA's do."

"I am glad to hear that Dee Dee, what a relief. A man like me would never have known that, I never go on the floor myself."

"Of course, not Mr. Vajeanya you are way too important for that."

"Please, Dee Dee call me Dick, and thank you."

"OK Dick!"

"There, that's much better." "Thank you, sir."

"You are more than welcome Dee Dee."

"I'm telling you Dick, CNA's hate each other. Every CNA thinks they are great, and everyone else sucks."

"Sounds like we have them right where we want them Dee Dee."

"You got it Dick. It is easy to brainwash them because they are full of shit. Now, I want to get our census up."

"Makes sense-is too me Dee Dee." "Ha ha, very funny Dick" "Thanks Dee Dee"

"No problem Dick. What I am going to do is start allowing prostitutes to live at FeudalCare."

"What! Are you kidding me Dee Dee?"

"No Dick, I am dead serious, hear me out ok." "I am all ears Dee Dee."

"We have a lot of dirty old men living here, correct?" "Yes Dee Dee, that is correct."

"And, they are always making unwanted sexual advances toward our female staff, right."

"Right again Dee Dee."

"We also have quite a few sex offenders here posing the same problem, am I right Dick?"

"Yes, you are Dee Dee."

"Well Dick, if we can get these dirty old men and sex offenders some action, we will stop getting in trouble with "THE STATE", with groping, and sexual harassment charges."

"It might work Dee Dee, it just might work."

"Trust me Dick, it will be great. There are also a lot of old men who complain they want to die, but can't."

"'Yea"

"Well Dick, a night with a HIV prostitute and they can stop procrastinating suicide. They will get their death wish. You know Dick I never understood why suicide does not have a 100 percent success rate. It is our job as loving healthcare providers to improve the odds and my plan is fool proof. It will do just that. And Dick, get a load of this they get to die with a smile on their face."

"Splendid Dee Dee, one thing though?" "What is that Dick?"

"We better make sure we change the bed linen every couple hours in the prostitute section."

"Why do we need the linen changed every couple of hours Dick?"

"I can just see one of those nut bag old ladies accidentally wandering into a prostitute room and lying down on the soiled sheets Dee Dee. Then waking up and claiming they are pregnant at age 90 because sperm got on their leg, or some other ridiculous bullshit."

"Good point Dick, even as an ex-prostitute I never thought of that. The student nurses can be in charge of changing the sheets, they don't get paid anyway, so it is free labor. They won't complain either because they are afraid of getting kicked out of class, Dick. The student nurses are a pain in the ass anyway, when you are trying to pass your own meds. They get in your way, they ask stupid questions, they have to check with you to make sure each med the put in the cup is ok etc. it is just dreadful. They are much better off making beds. It's not like they learn anything in clinicals anyway!"

"You Dee Dee, a God fearing, excellent Christian like yourself, and a nun, a former prostitute?"

"Yes Dick, regrettably so, but I let the Lord into my heart and became a born-again virgin, and the Lord has forgiven me."

"You are an inspiration to us all Dee Dee." "Thank you Dick"

"Well Dee Dee, at least we won't see charting in the nurse's notes saying patients states, haven't had sex in 10 years."

"Maybe Dick, we will get some of these old ladies too start being a little more active with the prostitutes here to push and spur them on. Some of them have not been laid since Columbus discovered America"

CHAPTER 3

Not Typical Procreation

For some unknown bizarre reason, anything of a sexual nature regarding nursing home residents or employees can defy the laws of nature.

Nurse Isabel Clingor was a bit out of the ordinary. She was extremely gullible and had no sense of humor. She was a nice person, but very melodramatic and flaky. She thrived on being one up on everybody. Every day was a crisis, every situation unbelievable, and everything that happened to her, was worse than anything that ever happened to anyone else.

If you had double bypass surgery, she had quadruple. If you had your gall bladder removed she had two gall bladders removed. If you found a dollar, she found five dollars. I could go on with a million other examples, but by now you get my drift.

Isabel was raised in a very old dilapidated building. She consumed a lot of lead from the peeling walls which affected her mental status, harmed her physically and ultimately made her unfit as a mom.

It destroyed her intestine so she needed a colostomy bag. Nothing bizarre about colostomy bags, thousands of people have them, and live quite normal lives.

Where Isabel's situation turns bizarre, is after she got married and became Mrs. Clingor. Like many newly- weds, the Clingor's were excited about starting a family. Much to The Clingor's shock and dismay their babies were not birthed or delivered in the conventional way. I am not referring to a c-section either this is something much more freakish!

Her babies, Paint Chips, Asbestos, and Little White and Nerdy were all born out of her colostomy bag! This resulted in serious problems for the babies, due to the fact that for nine months they were surrounded by fecal matter!

Asbestos never made it and died at birth.

Paint Chips was severely mentally impaired, all he could say was "my room", "Tylenol", and "can I go now". He aged at four times the rate of a normal human being and by the time he was twenty years old, was actually eighty. Ultimately though, it was Isabel's neglect as a parent that landed Paint Chips in FeudalCare as a resident.

Little White and Nerdy got off relatively unscathed. She had only a few minor quirks, really fucked up hair, dorkiness, breast implants that were always popping, she lived on a diet of Oreos, bacon, and Pepsi with tons of ice and she had a very annoying walk. She dragged her feet and stamped! Definitely not pick pocket or burglar material.

CHAPTER 4

Fish its What's for Dinner

FeudalCare hired a new nurse named Manute. He was nearly seven feet tall and thin as a needle. He was born in Somalia, Africa and was a huge prankster. He loved to play practical jokes.

I had previously mentioned how Isabel had no sense of humor. Manute was very sharp and picked up on this right away. One day a resident Mr. Scuddowski was out all day, from 7AM in the morning till 10PM at night. Mr. Scuddowski was not particularly fond of Isabel, because she was very bossy. In an attempt get on Mr. Scuddowski good side, she decided to have the kitchen set aside a try of fried fish for him. Isabel beamed with excitement as Mr. Scuddowski walked through the door!

"Good evening Mr. Scuddowski, my you look very scuddly clean shaven!"

'Thank you Isabel"

"You're welcome Mr. Scuddowski, I bet you are hungry?"
"No not really Isabel I just want to go to bed."

"But Mr. Scuddowski I had the kitchen set aside a plate of fried fish for you."

"Well, since you went through all that trouble Isabel, I guess I could eat something."

"Oh good, Mr. Scuddowski, I will go get it and heat it up for you."

"Thank you Isabel"

Isabel saunters off to the kitchen to get the fish all beaming with pride and self-righteousness! Much to her shock and dismay the fish dinner is completely devoured. Not just the fish, but the French Fries, cucumber salad, roll, and even the carton of milk!

"Manute"

"Yes Isabel, what is it"

"Do you know what happened to Mr. Scuddowski fish?"

"No Isabel I have no idea."

"Manute, I think that is the lowest down, underhanded, dirty, lousy thing anyone could do, to eat a resident's food."

"Oh, I agree with you Isabel. I feel so bad for you, you went through all that trouble to get that tray of food ready for Mr. Scuddowski and someone ate it. We got to get to the bottom of this! Should I call President Dee Dee?"

"I don't think that is necessary Manute, but I do appreciate your concern!"

"Well, it is the least I can do Isabel I feel so bad for you."

"Thank you Manute."

"You are welcome Isabel."

"Manute, I am going to question all the CNA's maybe they fed the food to another resident."

"I will try to find out if one of the residents knew the combination and snuck into the kitchen Isabel"

One half hour later. "Any luck Manute?"

"No Isabel, how about you?"

"Nope, none at all Manute, I will go tell Mr. Scuddowski the bad news."

"Mr. Scuddowski" "Yes Isabel"

"I have some bad news for you, someone ate your dinner." "Oh, that's Ok my daughter bought me a hamburger and some French Fries anyway, I did not even really want the fish, I just need the burger and fries heated up."

"I will heat it up for you Mr. Scuddowski."

"No Isabel, I want Manute to heat it up for me, that will give me some time to buy him a soda, and find a knife so I can cut this in half and give him half.

"That's not fair Mr. Scuddowski, I went through all the trouble of getting fish for you, I go out of my way to be nice to you, and you treat me like dirt. Manute does not do anything special for you, he probably ate your fish, and you are buying him a pop and giving him half your burger."

"It is not Manute's fault that he is sweeter than you Isabel." "AAAAAAAAAAAAAAAHHHHHHHHHHHHHH, Mr. Scuddowski you infuriate me!"

"Manute, I have a sneaking suspicion who ate Mr. Scuddowski's fish?" "Who Isabel" "You Manute"

"That is not true Isabel I would never do something that terrible to a resident."

"Yes, you would Manute."

"No Isabel, I think you ate it and you are trying to frame me. I'll get the phone Isabel."

"Who was that Manute"

"That was Mr. Scuddowski's daughter." "What did she want?"

"She wanted to know if her dad made it back safe."

"What did you tell her?"

"That Mr. Scuddowski was lost, that we have no idea what happened to him. We have five or six people out looking for him but that I don't think we are going to be able to find him."

"You didn't Manute, did you?"

"Yes, I did Isabel."

"Don't even start with me Manute, not after the stressful last three days I have had!"

CHAPTER 5
Ativan Not Just A Pill

As good as Manute was at pulling practical jokes, even he could not believe Isabel fell for this. All of us probably know someone who is the constant butt of practical jokes because they are always boohooing and wailing about it. If they would just let it go and laugh about it the jokes would stop, but because it bothers them so much, it encourages the prankster to continue. That was the situation with Manute and Isabel. Manute actually liked Isabel but he simply could not resist the opportunity to get her goat.

Such was the case with the plastic containers that the refrigerated intramuscular Ativan was kept in. Because there were so many residents on hall number two who needed intramuscular Ativan shots the small plastic container adequately could not hold them all.

Isabel was so proud of herself for going out and buying a bigger plastic box. One day at shift change Manute and Isabel were counting the refrigerated Ativan to make sure they were all present and accounted for.

"Isabel, what happened to your big plastic box for the Ativan on hall number two?"

"State (the regulation enforcers) was here and said all the boxes had to be the same size so I had to take it home." Manute laughed hysterically.

"What is so funny Manute?"'

"That wasn't State it was me. I took them out of the big box as a joke, you can put them back Isabel."

"Oh no Manute, President Dee Dee was here and she specifically told me it was State."

"Isabel President Dee Dee is on vacation, she wasn't even here this week it was me not State."

"I don't believe you Manute it was State." "OK Isabel if you say so."

"Well, if it is you Manute, you just lost yourself a good big plastic Ativan box."

"That is devastating news Isabel I hope someday I will be able to recover from it."

"I am not in the mood Manute, not after the stressful week I've had! Damn it, alright who is the asshole whole stole my cigarettes?"

I think it was that new C.N. A. Becca, the one who is giving up cigarettes for her kids, but is always bumming them.

"I think you are right Manute, there is a note in my empty cigarette pack."

"Isabel, I stopped by to borrow a few cigarettes, I'm broke and am quitting because it's a nasty habit, I hope you don't mind?

"What a minute, Becca does not even work tonight and this is not her handwriting MANUTE!!"

CHAPTER 6

A Mishap for Isabel's Daughter

It has been said that the apple doesn't fall far from the branch and that offspring have to bare the sins of their parents or something like that. Anyway, it's in the bible I think somewhere towards the middle or maybe the beginning or the end, who knows, but it's in the bible so it has to be true! I think?

Little White and Nerdy faced her own reproduction problems undoubtedly since she was Isabel's daughter. She actually loved two men and could not decide which one to marry, so she married them both. They both smelled like pee which was a strong turn-on for Little White and Nerdy. One was an elderly senior citizen gentleman named Tanner who although he still looked very dapper, had completely lost his mind. The other Rosco was a nurse at FeudalCare and in his early fifties.

As luck would have it Rosco and Tanner began fighting over who was the father of the child. There was only one way to settle this and that was to go on Jerry Springer and be DNA tested. This is where it gets weird, and I don't think there is anything in the bible about this. Although if there is it will be somewhere in the beginning, middle or end.

Turns out after DNA testing, the baby was both of theirs. Tanner was half the father and Rosco was the other half. One baby, two dads, unheard of, never before has there been a reported case in history of this happening, unless it's in the bible. But anything can happen when sex, procreation and offspring fall under the nursing home umbrella.

Little White and Nerdy had a normal delivery unlike Isabel so at least that went OK. And, Tanner and Rosco, because they had enough love in their heart for Little White and Nerdy were able to put aside their petty jealousies. While, they never became the best of friends they were civil to each other and both truly loved Little White and Nerdy.

The four of them Tanner, Rosco, Little White and Nerdy and baby Moby became the model for the new All-American Family! Possibly in an attempt to over compensate for the lack of care, love and affection Little White and Nerdy received growing up she really spoiled baby Moby. Every time he cried, screamed or hollered, Little White and Nerdy would pacify him with junk food. He grew up to weigh 500 pounds. His tremendous girth made his male genitalia shrivel up inside him. He was unable to urinate in a regular fashion and had to have a catheter 24/7. Hence, he became known as "Moby No Dick."

Despite all the odds and setbacks Moby faced in his life, he pulled himself up by his bootstraps (actually he had someone else do it, he could not reach them) and became a success story. He went on to become a head football coach at a major college university, and, almost won a national championship. Future Super Bowl MVP Nares Patent was robbed by the ref of a fantastic game winning catch in the end zone. Moby went on the Atkins Diet and lost so much weight, he was able to have his catheter removed and pee standing up!

CHAPTER 7

Labor is Killing Us

Dee Dee was bound and determined reduce the amount of money spent on labor!

"As far as labor is concerned Dick, what I have in mind, is to cut the work force in half on every shift."

"What do you mean?"

"For example, Dick, if we have 2 CNA's on each wing making $6 an hour. Multiply that by 4 wings, and $48 an hour in wages."

"I follow you so far Dee Dee."

"I knew you would Dick you are an extremely intelligent man!"

"Why thank you Dee Dee."

"My pleasure, if we cut down to one CNA per wing, times four wings at $6 an hour, you have $24 an hour in wages."

"I see Dee Dee, excellent we've effectively cut labor in half and doubled productivity, because now we have 1 CNA doing the work of 2."

"Exactly Dick"

"Won't the CAN's complain about being overworked?" "Are you kidding me Dick, I will tell them the same crock of shit we've been feeding them for years."

"What's that Dee Dee?"

"That the census is down and we need to make budgetary constraints. I will keep emphasizing how "lucky they are to have a job," that a lot of people are unemployed and not as fortunate as they are."

"Are you sure they will buy it Dee Dee?"

"Dick, remember when you were a kid, and your parents, or any adult for that matter kept telling you the same lie over and over again?"

"Like, liberals are great at spending other people money?" "Exactly Dick"

"Yea I remember that."

"Well, eventually you believed it because you heard it over and over and over again, like the failed hardware in our knee and hip replacement residents, it sticks, and you believed it, without even questioning it."

"Yes, Dee Dee I remember it like it was yesterday. Pop must have told me a million times the biggest mistake this country ever made was dumping Herbert Hoover in favor of Franklin Delano Roosevelt. Pop certainly did not have any failed hardware on his shoulders."

"Well Dick, CNA's are ignorant, they have the intellectual capacity of a very small child. They will believe anything we tell them if they here it enough!"

"Even that Ronald Reagan won the Cold War?" "Absolutely Dick, if a CNA knew what the Cold War was, they would believe it."

"Wow! Dee Dee, CNA's really are stupid, I did not think it was possible to be that dumb."

"Yes, they are Dick, we are so far superior to them it is not even funny."

"Excellent Dee Dee I am sure glad I thought of you and only you to be FeudalCare's next President." "Thank you, sir, I am very glad I took the job."

CHAPTER 8

The Only Thing Dumber than a CNA is a Nurse

"Dee Dee, remember before you left FeudalCare there was a definite hierarchy?"

"I'm not sure I know what you mean Dick?" "Well, there was a chain of command Dee Dee."

"Oh, you mean that the CNA's new their place Dick."

"Yes Dee Dee, they realized they were on the bottom of the food chain."

'Well Dick my fellow nurses back then like Tilly and Tabitha as well as President Screwem and Vice President Howe, would not let them forget it."

"Right you drummed it into their head every step of the way Dee Dee."

"It is not like that anymore Dick?"

"Oh no Dee Dee, not at all FeudalCare has really gone to hell in a hen basket."

"How so, Dick

"Oh, Dee Dee there are so many areas I don't know where to start"

"I know you are upset Dick, just take a deep breath, relax, and pick a topic, any topic and just begin there."

"It doesn't have to be the most important Dee Dee?" "Nope, anything you like Dick."

"Ok, let's see now Dee Dee, oh, bed alarms." "Go ahead Dick."

"Well Dee Dee, we all know bed alarms do not prevent falls, or diminish their seriousness."

"Uh, huh Dick, residents have a right to fall. That is until they actually do fall. Then we blame the CNA's."

"Precisely Dee Dee",

"I remember a resident who would set off his bed alarm on purpose, Dick."

"Why is that Dee Dee?"

"Two reasons actually Dick. He said it sounded like a seal and he liked that. The second being the CNA's came to his room much quicker if they thought he fell, then if he used the regular call light."

"Now that you mention it Dee De, I remember a supervisor telling me about a resident who would shut off his alarm, get up and go to the bathroom, then turn it back on when he got back in bed."

"On another instance Dee Dee I told a supervisor to fire a CNA for abuse but off the record it was funny as hell! A resident would set off his bed alarm to have his urinal emptied. Every time the CNA would say, excuse me sir, would you mind if I emptied your urinal? The poor old demented goof would absolutely fly off the handle! He'd scream, do you have shit for brains, I just asked you to do that. The Aide would reply calmly, oh sorry sir I did not know that, my bad. It was hilarious Dee Dee!"!

"That is funny Dick, off the record of course."

"Of course, Dee Dee, and those vital signs, there only purpose is to fuck with the Aides."

"Yea Dick bed alarms and vital signs totally fuck the Aides, I love it. Come to think of it, every rule was designed to fuck with the Aides, charting, 2-hour bed checks, vital signs, input and outputs, BM's etc. they are all meant to fuck with the CNA's, so what is your point Dick?"

"Sorry Dee Dee, I need to digress here for a minute." "Ok Dick"

"Remember how those bed alarms would constantly go off fifty to sixty times a night, even though the resident was lying peacefully sound asleep on the bed?"

"Yea Dick, I remember, that is funny."

"The CNA's would get so frustrated, running in and out of those rooms fifty or sixty times a night."

"Yea I do Dick."

"They would never disconnect the alarms though, because they were scared to death if a resident did fall, they would get in trouble Dee Dee."

"Invariably the resident would fall anyway, and we'd blame the CNA's and either write them up, or fire them, Dick. They actually believed it was their fault, and that they were responsible for the fall. That is too funny!"

"And, we would get off Scott- free, when the state or FBI came to investigate, President Dee Dee! The Aides took the fall for us every time."

"What is your concern about bed alarms then Dick?" "Well Dee Dee, the way it used to be bed alarms were the perfect scam. Oh, sure once in a great while a CNA would outsmart us and just answer the alarm an hour or two later when he did rounds, but that was very seldom. Now, they just shut them off"

"What! They just shut them off. Oh my God Dick when I was here a CNA would be scared to death to shut off a bed alarm!"

"Not any more Dee Dee, this left leaning Phil Donahue type let them in on the gig. They don't believe it anymore, bed alarms no longer scare CNA's."

"That is just awful Dick, awful. I will reinstate "the gig" and if any CNA refuses to believe it, they can hit the road. I will just hire some other nit wit to replace him or her."

"That is the spirit Dee Dee, I am getting all excited again." "Calm yourself Dick, I know you think I am attractive, but let's stick to business Ok?" "Ok Dee"

"What is next on your mind Dick?"

"Gays in the nursing home, is next on the agenda Dee Dee." "Wow, Dick isn't that ironic when Bill Clinton became president one of his first orders of business was gays in the military and one of my first orders of business as President of FeudalCare is gays in the nursing home."

"I sure hope you handle the problem better than Clinton did Dee Dee."

"Of course, Dick, Clinton did not have my moral fiber and intestinal fortitude. I am an intelligent God-fearing woman."

"I don't want to sound prejudice Dee Dee because I am not. My mom's, best friends, dad had a cousin who knew a gay person. So I speak from experience, I am an expert on the topic of homosexuality. I am sure he was a nice man and I don't want to sound unkind, but gays give me the CREEPS!" "Speaking of experts Dick, my dad had a friend Bert Lajose, who died of renal failure." "I'm sorry to hear that Dee Dee."

"Never mind that Dick, my question for you, is when he died, did he become an ex-bert?"

"I suppose he did Dee Dee."

"Dick, if God wanted us to be gay, he would have created Adam and Steve, not Adam and Eve."

"That is hysterical Dee Dee I've never heard that before, that is too good. I can tell you are a very intelligent woman."

"Thank you sir"

"You are welcome Dee Dee."

"What do you we propose we do about the gay thing Dee Dee?"

"Well Dick, I can spot a flamer a mile away so my first order of business is to cut off the homo process at the source. We will not hire anyone who even remotely looks gay! I realize some heterosexuals look gay but hey that is there fault, we can't afford to take the chance and hire them."

"Excellent Dee Dee I agree wholeheartedly but even as intelligent as the two of us are, we can't pick out every limp wristed weenie, some are bound to fall through the cracks."

"Ha ha ha fall through the cracks, boy that is hysterical you are really on a roll today sir!"

Vajeanya pauses clueless as too what Dee Dee means, fakes a laugh to save face, and then gets the pun.

"Oh, ha ha, Dee Dee, what are we going to do if a fudgepacker accidentally gets hired?"

"Dick I am going to wiretap the whole building and if any guy so much as mentions fashion design, or hairstyling they are out of here!"

"That is great Dee Dee You've been on the job only a few hours, and already you are making significant in-roads in restoring FeudalCare to its glory days!"

"In roads, Dick, and we are talking about gays. Oh Dick, you are a sly one."

"Oh yes, Dee Dee yes, thank you." "You are welcome sir."

"And, I will be on the lookout if anyone touches my butt or even so much as makes eye contact with me." "Good for you sir"

"And, no one better use that lispy voice around me or they will never set foot in FeudalCare again."

"That is the spirit Dick."

"But, we can't just come out and fire them for being gay. This isn't like the good old days when you could fire a fudgepacker just for being queer."

"You are right Dee Dee we can't do that anymore." "Today Dick, we need to make up some politically correct, sanitized reason for dismissal."

"I know what you mean Dee Dee, we try so hard to be politically correct, and follow procedures, communication becomes harder and harder. To the point it paralyzes us, what are you going to do Dee Dee?

"How about failure to abide by company policy, Dick" "That is perfect Dee Dee, it is so plan, generic, and covers such a wide variety of areas, it won't be apparent we fired them for being gay."

"And best of all Dick, no attorney can sink their teeth into any possible injustice. It will have them completely fooled."

"Effective immediately Dee Dee this policy is being implemented. Off the record of course (nudge nudge wink wink)."

"Of course, sir (nudge nudge wink wink)."

CHAPTER 9

President Dee Dee Hits The Floor Running

"Jacintha!!" "Sister Dee Dee!!"

(Jacintha and Dee Dee leap into each other's arms)

"Oh my God Dee Dee, it is so good to see you! I can't believe it, what are you doing here?"

"You did not hear the news Jacintha?" "No, what news is that Dee Dee?"

"I'm the new FeudalCare Administrator Jacintha!" "No way Dee Dee!

"Yes, way Jacintha"

"Oh my God Dee Dee that is too good to be true, I can't believe it!"

"Well believe it because it's true Jacintha!" "That's just wonderful Dee Dee!"

"I know, Jacintha I am so excited."

"But, I thought you devoted your life to God, doing missionary work in India?

"I did and don't get me wrong, I loved doing the Lord's work in India but FeudalCare and I are like soul mates. I was really torn but you can't fight who you are and FeudalCare will always be my first love. I am sure the Lord understands and wants me to be happy."

I am sure too Dee Dee, I am so glad to have you back. I thought I'd never see you again!"

"Likewise, Jacintha"

"Dee Dee have you seen the beautiful Memorial to President Screwem and Vice President Howe in the smoke hut?"

No, I haven't Jacintha."

Just as Dee Dee and Jacintha were about to head out to enjoy a healthcare workers favorite pastime, a situation arose for Dee Dee to show off her abundance of estrogen and put her authority on display. Mr. Alonso was roaming the halls fully dressed, and it was only two thirty in the morning. Dee Dee waddled back to the intercom behind the nurse's station and grabbed the microphone.

"Please have the Broadway Unit CNA report to the nurse's station regarding Thomas Alonso."

Little did President Dee Dee Kuntz realize, she just committed a class A Felony, the most serious of all HIPPA violations, violating a resident's privacy by publicly announcing his name over the intercom, luckily, no one was aware of the law, otherwise President Dee Dee most certainly in have been tossed in the HIPPA Jail.

A stunned and very sheepish CNA Sharon emerged from a room on Broadway, where she was attending to another resident."

"Yes ma'am, what is the matter?" "Did you get Mr. Alonso dressed?" "Yes ma'am, why?"

Angrily President Dee Dee pounds her fist on the nurse's station and yells, "no one, I mean no one, gets a resident at FeudalCare up and dressed before 4 A.M. Do you hear me?"

"I understand Ma'am, but Mr. Alonso was already up, and wandering the halls naked. Since he is on my list of people to get up and dressed, it only made sense, to get him dressed!"

"If you put him back in bed Sharon, why was he roaming the halls?"

"He got back up again."

President Dee Dee went berserk again, and pounded the desk once more. "Did you hear me, no one, I mean no one, gets a FeudalCare resident up and dressed before 4 A.M. do you understand me?"

In a flash Sharon's fear and intimidation of Dee Dee resided and anger set in.

"Ma'am, that is absolutely ridiculous. I could understand if Mr. Alonso was sound asleep and I woke him up to get dressed, but he was awake naked and wandering the halls. It would have been utterly stupid to put his pajamas back on, then take them off in an hour and a half, and get him back up."

"Are you questioning me young lady?"

"No ma'am, I am just using common sense that is all." "I've had enough of your attitude Sharon, punch out and go home."

"No!"

"What did you say?"

"I said no, if you want me out of here, you need to throw me out."

President Dee Dee got on the phone to call security.

"I have heard all about you President Dee Dee, you call security and have me fired, and I will take you down with me."

Dee Dee had a stunned look on her face.

"On second thought Sharon, he was up anyway, and you had to get him dressed in an hour or so, so I suppose what you did is alright."

"Thank you ma'am" "You are welcome"

"Jacintha, let's go smoke and check out the hut." "Good, I need one"

"Likewise, Jacintha"

Dee Dee it is absolutely beautiful! Both President Screwem and Vice President Howe have their ashes enshrined in a beautiful bullet proof case. It is so moving, like their bowels were."

"Sounds like it, I can't wait to see it. I really need a cigarette. This is a perfect time to check it out and catch up on old times."

"Great Dee Dee, you don't need to twist my arm to get me to take a cigarette break, I love to smoke."

"Dee Dee, we are caring on Screwem and Howe's legacy and paying tribute to them every time we go out to the hut and smoke."

"That we are Jacintha, they were two of the all-time greats." "Amen Dee Dee, amen, great executives, great smokers advocates, and great Christians'

CHAPTER 10
The Devil Made Me Do It

President Dee Dee is about to do something she has not done in her 22 years of nursing. No, I don't mean take a shower she does that at least once a month, well maybe a little longer, after spending a few years in India. When the people on the mission greeted her by saying Hi Jean, she either thought it was a term of affection or they did not know her name was Dee Dee. She never got the hint it was a reference to her body odor. She is not going on a diet either, she has done that thousands of times. No, Nurse Dee is about to answer a call light. Before you get all excited and ahead of yourself, thinking President Dee Dee is finally developing a sense of compassion and humility, think again!

Seems a television set is very loud, and is blaring out obscene and blasphemous utterances. The sound was coming from the room of none other than Super Bowl MVP Nares Patent. Nares is in The Rehabilitation Unit to recuperate from grom surgery.

"Mr. Patent. What on earth are you watching? This is a Christian Healthcare Facility and I am a religious and God fearing woman, such language is highly inappropriate and will not be tolerated!"

"Shut the fuck up nurse! I want to hear my tape after I was presented the MVP Trophy for winning The Super Bowl."

"Ladies and Gentleman this is Robbie Tussin standing here with Super Bowl MVP Nares Patent. Nares tell me how you feel right now?"

"I want to thank Satan for this tremendous victory, through Him, all things are possible!"

"Turn that tape off this instant Mr. Patent, I forbid you to listen to that garbage."

Of course, President Dee Dee, the world-renowned hypocrite, is drawn to the tape like a crowd to a terrible traffic accident. She watches and listens intently to every second of it. After all, President Dee Dee is the type of woman who would be smoking a joint in her house, and call the cops because her neighbors were playing poker.

"Nares, you have some very unorthodox views, would you clarify yourself for our audience?"

"Well, before I accepted Satan into my heart I was a sniveling coward, like our former President Jorge Hedge, afraid of my own shadow."

"Wait a minute Nares, why is President Hedge a coward?" "Because Robbie, he has no problem sending young gullible kids off to die in a senseless war, so he, his candy ass Vice President Nick Linkey, and his cronies in the oil industry can reap huge profits. Yet, he is opposed to letting a terminally ill person suffering terribly the right to die with dignity." "Anyway Robbie, I was a sniveling coward, afraid of my own shadow. I constantly worried about SIN! I was completely paralyzed from having any fun. I stayed locked in my room praying, offering penance and telling myself how unworthy I was. I was a miserable wretch with no confidence convinced my family and I were going to hell. I got a staph infection in my knee from praying. I weighed 90 pounds from fasting trying to make sure I would enter the pearly gates."

"Let's pause thirty seconds for a public service announcement from Father Sinalot."

"I shudder to think how many Adolph Hitler's, Charles Manson's, and Saddam Hussein's would be walking the streets today, had it not been for Roe vs Wade. Keep abortion legal!! Now back to our regularly scheduled programming."

"How did you overcome this affliction Nares?"

"Well a representative from the church of SAD randomly knocked on my door."

"If you were afraid of sinning, why did you answer the door?"

"He said the word church, so I figured I was safe Robbie." "Oh Ok"

"We interrupt this broadcast for a special announcement.

Are you a bitter, malicious, petty, vile single mom with dysfunctional kids? Do you hate life? Consider a career in nursing!! Now back to our regularly scheduled broadcast."

"He said he was a member of the church of SAD." "What is that?"

"Satanic Assembly of the Devil"

"Nares turn that blasphemous talk off immediately! It is a direct insult to Almighty God and will not be tolerated in a Christian nursing home."

"Shove it up your ass President Dee Dee!"

Of course, President Dee Dee continues to listen to fuel her righteous indignation.

"Robby, it was not until I accepted the Devil that I found any enjoyment in my life." "What do you mean?"

"Well, I began to loosen up and have some fun."

"How so, Nares?"

"I started going to bars and meeting women."

"Wow!!"

"I started to have a social life and got the damn notion of sin out of my head."

"Nares, you realize this is quite controversial and is not going to go over well with a lot of people."

"I don't give a flying fuck!!"

Nares is immediately censored and a loud beep is transmitted from the screen.

Angrily Nurse Dee storms out of the room. She is hell bent on punishing Nares Patent and expelling him from the facility. That is if Nares does not get so pissed off at President Dee Dee first, and try to escape by pulling a "Shawshank Redemption" with his cast and chisel his way out!

Her appeal is a no go because of the Supreme Court's decision to allow people a right to their own religious opinion.

An irate President Dee Dee vows revenge.

CHAPTER 11

There's Gonna Be Big Changes Around Here

After two weeks on the job President Dee Dee realized the staff was just horrendous. Rehabilitating this bunch of losers was going to take every ounce of her superb nursing skills. A lesser nurse would have at best cleaned house or at worst been panic stricken and given up. President Dee Dee had worked miracles before. She was bound and determined to rebuild the staff in her own image.

She was appalled at the expensive of giving showers and baths. Still fuming over the Supreme Court's decision in the Nares Patent case, she attacked the business of implementing a new shower and bath policy with a vengeance.

Joey was all excited going to visit Grandma Seizure at the Nursing Home. His sister Fibrosis on the other hand wants no part of it and is vehemently opposed and protesting vigorously. "I don't want to go Momma old people stink and spread diseases. I don't want my clothes smelling like old people." "That's only if they touch you Fibrosis, and mommy doesn't like when you talk that way honey."

"But it's true."

"That's enough Fibrosis."

"Yes Mommy."

Joey's excitement quickly turned to terror upon entering the facility. He was greeted by old lady Melony who started chasing him around in her wheel chair the minute he set foot in the door.

"Come to Gramma sweetie!" "AH AH AH AH"

"Mommy is here honey, that lady did not mean to scare you, she just wanted to give you a hug and a kiss, and to be your friend."

"I don't want to be her friend she is gross and has no teeth. She has funny looking old people syndrome."

"Honey, that's not nice, now be a good boy and mommy will give you a lollipop."

"A cherry lollipop, mommy" "Yes Joey, cherry"

"Ok Mommy"

Just as they were about to walk into Grandma Seizures room, an irate female CNA charges out of an adjacent room with a dripping wet diaper in her hand.

"Jester, did you get Mrs. Franks up this morning?" "Yes I did Meg, why?"

"You left this on the floor Jester."

Meg angrily slams the diaper to the ground and lashes out. "I don't clean up anyone else's shit!"

Mrs. Franks is still screaming about having her soiled diaper removed.

"Stop ripping off my good clothes, my daughter does not have money like that to keep buying me new clothes."

"Joey, come back here honey, let's go see Grandma Seizure. No honey, don't stick peanut butter and bubble gum in that old man's trachea, that's not nice. Come here honey, that's a good boy."

"GOD DAME YOU", hollers old lady Karen as a spit ball lands on her nose.

"Fibrosis, stop shooting spitballs at that elderly lady" "GOD DAME YOU", as one last spit ball flies out of Fibrosis straw and lands right in the middle of Karen's forehead.

Gladys is shocked as she enters Grandma Seizures room, and hears here yelling for a Tylenol Patch and a house cigarette. She ran out of her Camel filter-less. Joey was too busy looking at the goldfish doing all types of weird flips in his bowl to even notice Grandma Seizure's distress. He asks his sister.

"Fibrosis do you think the goldfish has "old timer's disease" like the old lady chasing me in the wheel chair?"

"No Joey I don't think so."

"Why not"

"The fish doesn't have a diaper on over its pants or a bra on over its blouse."

"Fish don't wear clothes or diapers Fibrosis."

"See, that's why it does not have "old timers'" disease" "Oh Ok Fibrosis I guess you are right."

"Ma'am, what are you doing to my mother?"

The woman was about to answer, but was interrupted as Grandma Seizures roommates bed alarm went off and made a ringing sound. Her roommate picks up her orthopedic shoe and places it by her ear.

The roommate pipes out a loud, "hello"

"My name is Hilary I am a retired nurse doing volunteer work."

"More like a retarded nurse if you ask me," mumbles Gladys.

"I'm just doing my job ma'am, today is your moms bath day, so I am getting her a cleaned up."

"With hand sanitizer, that is alcohol based, my mother has very sensitive skin and many sores, you are hurting her, can't you see her writhing in pain?"

"If you ask me ma'am, your mom is kind of a wimp. The hand sanitizer has only been marinating on her skin for an hour. She is not in that much pain. Besides ma'am, I am just doing my job."

"There must be some kind of mistake Hilary."

"Oh no Gladys, there is no mistake, there is no room for error in the nursing profession."

"When did start giving bed baths with hand sanitizer? My mom has been at FeudalCare for five years and has never had a bath with hand sanitizer."

"Effective immediately, complete bed baths are required to be given in hand sanitizer."

"Hilary, no one in their right mind would implement a policy requiring bed baths in hand sanitizer, unless they are a complete moron."

"You must know our new administrator President Dee Dee then."

"No, I don't, why would you say that?"

"You said moron Gladys, and moron epitomizes President Dee Dee."

"No, I don't Hilary, but I am going to make it a point to do so."

"Gladys President Dee Dee is like a fungus."

"How so"

"She just won't go away, no matter how hard you try. Just when you think she is gone, she pops right back up again."

"Wasn't she a nurse here before?"

"Yes, she was. Prior to that, she owned a liquor store. Her first career made people sick, then she became a nurse and made people even sicker, then after completely destroying their physical health, she becomes a "Godfreak" so she can save the heathens souls before her nursing tactics kill them. Even India could not contain her. "India?"

Just before the retired nurse was about to explain India, an agency nurse popped her head in the door. She just finished going through the motions performing CPR (slow code) on an individual she did not particularly care for. The man died, but that was no big deal. She needed a pen to chart that she tried to perform some type of activity to alleviate the situation.

"Excuse me, I don't mean to interrupt, but I've lost my pen and I need to chart that I performed CPR on a cardiac arrest patient."

"Did the patient die?"

"Yes?

"Damn what a shame." "That he died?"

"Hell no, I don't give a shit about that, but this is the only pen I got. What a minute thank goodness we had another death last night so I can go ahead and give you this pen."

"What does someone dying last night have to do with you being able to give me a pen?"

"That means there will be one of those phony, cheesy, condolence cards in the lobby for the staff to sign."

"What?"

"It is a chance the for staff to bullshit about how much they loved the deceased, and how much they are going to miss them, even though they did not know them. Anyway, there will be a pen by the card, so I can give you this one and take the one by the card. A death is so wonderful when you need a pen. Sorry Gladys where were we now?"

"India"

"Oh yea, she worked at FeudalCare for years as a regular nurse, when she suddenly found "The Big Guy" upstairs and became a born-again virgin. She left FeudalCare (for good supposedly) to became a nun and went over to India to do missionary work. She wanted to rub the pagan's nose in the dirt for not being devout Christians like she is. But, wouldn't you know it, FeudalCare was always her first love and when the opportunity to become the next Administrator reared its ugly head, she grabbed the chance by the throat."

"Well her dream job became every resident and their family's nightmare Hilary?"

"Isn't that the truth ma'am, it became every nurse and C.N.A's nightmare too."

"What in the world would possess her to want to give baths with hand sanitizer?"

"The bottom line, ma'am, the bottom line"

"How so"

"It is a lot cheaper to spread a little hand sanitizer over a person's body and let it air dry than it is to spend money on water, soap, and towels."

"Well, Nurse Dee will be hearing from the state and my attorney."

"You GO GIRL, but I must warn you don't get your hopes up that President Dee Dee will face any disciplinary actions."

"Why not?"

"She is like a swarm of cockroaches a nuclear holocaust couldn't keep her from coming back."

"Joey would you like to go to Red Lobster for lunch?" "No mommy I want to eat at the FeudalCare Cafeteria the food is so yummy!"

"What about you Fibrosis?"

"I want to eat at the FeudalCare Cafeteria too. I want some of that smushed up Peru food like Grandma Seizure eats. You know, the kind that is so soft, she can even take out her teeth to eat."

"That is pureed food honey!" "Well, that is what I want."

"You kids are ridiculous, you would rather go to the FeudalCare Cafeteria and eat that junk than go to a nice restaurant?"

"Yes mommy," replies Joey," tonight's special is the buffet or the feeding tube."

"You two sure will be a cheap date."

"Why mommy", interjects Joey and Fibrosis at the same time.

"You would rather eat pureed food at the FeudalCare cafeteria than go to a fancy restaurant." "Yep", says Fibrosis

"Me too", says Joey

"When you two grow up and get married your spouses will save a bundle of money on food."

"No, they won't", says Fibrosis.

"Why not honey"

"I hate boys, they are yucky!"

"And I am never growing up", says Joey.

"Kids"

CHAPTER 12

Hands Off Policy

A knot formed in CNA Boyd's stomach when he received a call from President Dee Dee to come in on his day off concerning a very serious matter. Boyd has Obsessive Compulsive Disorder. He tends to torment himself over trivial matters that are not even his fault. Where others would dismiss things as pure nonsense and forget about it, Boyd would ruminate for days on end. Nervously Boyd showered, dressed and got in his car to head off and see President Dee Dee.

"Good morning Boyd"

"Good morning President Dee Dee that is a lovely pants suit you have on."

"Why thank you Boyd that is so sweet of you to say."

President Dee Dee not being very smart forgets herself and immediately reaches for a cigarette hoping Boyd's will be a gentleman and light it. Before making a complete ass of herself she regains her composure and remembers the business at hand.

"Boyd, do you know why I called you here today?" "I haven't the faintest idea."

"Are you sure?"

"Because I dumped ice cubes on Hal?" "Why would you do that?"

"Too get him out of bed. Otherwise he won't budge." "You actually did that to Hal!"

"Oh my God no, of course not, I would never do that to Hal, I love him like he was a member of my own family."

"Then why did you mention it."

"Look Dee Dee I have no idea what I did wrong. I am just making random arbitrary guesses."

"Oh, well it is a good thing for you that it's not true, otherwise you'd be in worse trouble than you already are."

"What kind of trouble am I in?" "I forgot."

"Then I'm off the hook and free to go?"

"No, you are not off the hook at best you are getting fired at worst criminal charges will be pressed against you."

"Oh My God what for" "You tell me?"

"Imitating resident's voices?" "You do that?"

"Oh, for heaven's sake of course not, these residents are flesh and blood human beings just like you and I, to imitate them would be mean and cruel!"

"Why do you keep bringing these things up then Boyd, if you don't do them?"

"Because I am flabbergasted and have no earthly idea what I did wrong!"

"Are you sure?"

"Yes of course I'm sure, I give up, what did I do?"

"Mrs. Parson wants to file sexual harassment charges against you."

"What, what for?"

"She said that while you were getting her dressed, you fondled her breasts."

"Oh, for God Sake I had no choice, it was unavoidable."

"Why?"

"She had a mastectomy and insists on wearing a bra and prosthesis. How am I going to put on her bra and fake boob without out touching her tits?"

"Don't use the word boob or tit again Boyd, it is very disrespectful."

"Sorry ma'am you are right, prosthesis." 'That is better Boyd, thank you."

"You are welcome President Dee Dee."

"Boyd, you could have been more respectful and at least used a Kleenex, so there would have been a barrier between your hands and her breasts."

"Oh my God no way President Dee Dee, don't even say that."

Why not"

"Are you kidding Dee Dee, old people love Kleenex. If she even so much as thought I was going to waste a Kleenex she'd have died of cardiac arrest. I don't care what you say Old Boyd is not going to have a murder on his hands."

"Alright then, how about gloves, couldn't you have used them?"

"I tried Dee Dee, I really did but it's literally impossible to put the real boob and the fake boob in the bra, and have it fit right, without using your bare hands. It is like trying to type with mittens on."

"There you go again using the word boob." "Sorry breasts."

"I am warning you Boyd, use that word one more time and you definitely will be fired."

"Yes ma'am, it won't happen again."

"See that it doesn't OK, well, I suppose since you didn't enjoy it, you didn't enjoy it right?"

"Of course, I did not enjoy it Dee Dee!" "You did not get aroused at all?"

"No, Dee Dee I did not get aroused." "So, it was strictly business Boyd?"

"Of course, it was strictly business, Mrs. Parson's real boob is all spongy, squishy and yucky! And, the fake boob is a real pain in the ass to insert properly, the whole thing really bites."

"Boyd, I warned you!"

"Yes, ma'am it is just a habit I will really try to break it. Am I off the hook now?"

"Well, not exactly." "Now what"

"Mrs. Parson's says you raped her."

"The lady is lunatic Dee Dee she yells that even when the girls get her dressed. I've been married twenty years and never even cheated on my wife, but if I did it sure wouldn't be with a ninety-three-year-old woman!"

"I guess you are right Boyd." "Now am I free to go Dee Dee?"

"There is another sexual harassment complaint against you."

"By who"

"CNA Rita she feels very uncomfortable around you." "That's ridiculous President Dee Dee."

"Well, she is intimidated to work with a male."

"It's not my fault my dad shot out a Y chromosome." "That is enough Boyd."

"Rita is full of shit, why just last week, she asked me if I wanted to go to breakfast."

"Maybe she is just young and naive."

"Young and naive, out of a clear blue sky, she told me she wanted to have boobs like Halle Barry."

"There you go with that word again."

"That one doesn't count President Dee Dee I was just repeating her words."

"Alright, Boyd I will give you a pass on that one." "Unprovoked she even showed me her Bugs Bunny tattoo Dee Dee."

"Oh, do you want to see my Tweetie Bird tattoo?" "Not really President Dee Dee."

"Oh well yes umm umm that would be inappropriate. Tell you what I will do Boyd, I will ask the other female nurses and CNA's if they are afraid of you and if you are sexually harassing them, if they say no you will be clear on this account as well."

"You mean there is more?" "I am afraid so Boyd."

"This is ridiculous if this was not so tragic it would be comical. What now?"

"Well, Nurse Sherri said you had a CRAZED look in your eye when dealing with resident Salemo. She said it was the most terrifying thing she'd ever seen in her life, she was absolutely petrified."

"Petrified of me."

"Yes, of you."

"The woman has been in prison and something I did is the most terrifying thing she has ever seen?"

"That is what she said."

"If that doesn't beat all that must have been one wimpy prison"

"She said you were abusive to Mr. Salemo."

"Abusive! First off that man was in the mob he wrote the book on abusive. That nut walked into Mr. Fitzpatrick's room and stole his walker while his grandson was visiting. They were upset, so I got the walker back, but it was a struggle."

"How did you handle the situation?"

"I handled the situation with great diplomacy and tact, Dee Dee."

"*Go on*"

"Well Mr. Fitzpatrick's grandson came out of his room and told me his grandfather was very upset because a crazy man barged into his room and stole his walker. I did not see Mr. Salemo do this because I was getting the two ex-military men

General's Malaise and Soreness, off the toilet, God old people love to go to the bathroom!"

"That is enough Boyd I am getting tired of your disrespectful and rude comments. One more time and you are fired!"

"Yes ma'am"

"Now get to the point."

"Ok, I calmly approached Mr. Salemo and very politely asked him if I could please have Mr. Fitzpatrick's walker back."

"What happened then?"

"Mr. Salemo began spitting at me. He tried to punch and kick me as I went to get the walker back."

"What happened next?"

"I gave Mr. Fitzpatrick's grandson the walker and got Mr. Salemo a diet soda (diabetes compliance you know) he was happy as a lark. He forgot all about the situation and I did not give it another thought. Actually, I was quite proud of myself."

"Why so?"

"Well, last time Mr. Salemo got out of hand, the charge nurse had to call the police to contain him, and the nurse was so upset she wound up quitting. I handled the situation without getting any cops involved."

"You have a point Boyd I am going to let you off with a verbal warning and a coaching. I will document that I discussed this matter with you, and you will not be suspended or fired. Please be careful after this Boyd, and watch yourself when you are out on the floor."

"You are right Dee Dee not everyone is as good as person as you are and has our best interest at heart."

"Thank you, Boyd, unlike me a lot of people pretend to love the residents but only do so to make themselves look good at someone else's expense."

"That is what I admire about you President Dee Dee, you would never do that you genuinely care."

"Yes, Boyd I do, it is plain to see from our conversation that you are an extremely intelligent and perceptive man and this is all just one big misunderstanding. I'll tell you what, I am going to rip up your verbal warning and forget about the whole incident, you are free to go."

"You mean it President Dee Dee?" "I certainly do! You are free to go."

"Thank you, President Dee Dee, you are the best!" "I know, you are welcome, goodbye Boyd." "Good bye President Dee Dee."

Despite President Dee Dee's promise, Boyd was fired the next day. This came as no surprise to Boyd. He knew taking President Dee Dee at her word was about as successful as sweeping dirt under a rug. The shit comes out the other end.

Even though he was innocent of all charges, she just could not stomach the lewd language Boyd used throughout the conversation, the constant references to boobs and all. She grabbed Christianity by neck and rammed it down Boyd's throat all the way to the unemployment line!

CHAPTER 13

The Burns Unit

Anyone can run a top-flight inspection with advance warning. Even someone as stupid as your beloved author could get a I 00 percent on an exam if he had all the answers.

President Dee Dee did not become President of FeudalCare by being a dummy. Usually she is calm, cool, and collected, except when she panics. President Dee Dee was positive FeudalCare was in "tip top shape" for the upcoming state inspection. The Natzi's come once a year! She would have totally "freaked" if she got wind of this!

A crazed nurse Carol, was going to show Beth, a student nurse, how to do physical assessment. Beth was on cloud nine, a resident did not want a student nurse taking care of him, but Beth did it anyway, and got away with it. She came running down the hall yelling.

"Hooray, hooray, whoopee, whoopee, wee haa, wee haa, high five Carol, high five."

"What is it Beth, what is going on?"

"I gave a shot and an aspirin to a resident, who did not even want it. Yes! Yes! Yes!"

"Way to go Beth you are incredible. You did such a great job, I'm going to give you two free tickets to clean the break-room on your day off! Shit, I forgot my flashlight."

"How are you going to see how the resident's eyes react to light Carol?"

"Don't worry Beth I got matches in my pocket."

She strikes the match and puts it by the patient's eyes. Accidentally the flame touches the resident's hair. WHOOSH! Her whole body is engulfed in flames!

"Damn it Beth, I forgot old people hate to bathe! Her hair is so fuckin greasy the match ignited it!"

"It is not just her hair that is greasy Carol she has her whole body covered with Vaseline".

"Oh, yea Beth, I forgot, she thinks that if she keeps her skin moisturized and drinks skim milk, she will live forever.

"Why does she want to live forever, Carol?"

"She says she has seen every film on the American Film Institute's top 100 movies, Beth."

"So what Carol?"

"Well, she is afraid if she dies, she will forget about all the movies, Beth."

"Whatever!"

"Oblivious to the burning human being right before for her eyes, Mrs. Johnlove asks."

"Beth honey, could you get me the bed pan, I need to go stinky. And, there is no toilet paper on the roll next to my bed." "Mrs. Johnlove can't you see we are in an emergency here Mrs. Puff is on fire!"

"That is not my fault Beth, and a still need to go stinky, it is your fault for giving me that prune juice this morning and causing my diarrhea!"

"Mrs. Johnlove if you don't shut up, you are going to get an excrement day."

The Bur

"What is that?"

"It is a punishment for not shutting up you will lie in feces and urine all day."

"I am telling President Dee Dee you said that Beth."

"Mrs. Johnlove, at the rate your roommate is burning, you won't be able to tell President Dee Dee anything, because we are all going up in flames."

"I still say it your fault Beth and Carol, for giving me all that prune juice."

Carol intervenes, "Mrs. Johnlove you asked for the prune juice to relieve you constipation, besides there is a FIRE going on can't you see that?"

"That's not my problem and I still need the bed pan."

"For the last time Mrs. Johnlove if we don't get this fire put out you will never need the bed pan again now shut up!!"

"Oh you people!"

"Wait a minute Beth I got an idea." "What Carol?"

"Stick the bed pan under her Beth, but make sure it is her bed pan and not Mrs. Puff's or she will have a fit." "Why Carol?"

"Mrs. Johnlove has a bed pan addiction Beth!! She loves the bed pan so much she has her own personalized bed pan, if she doesn't use it, she goes through withdrawals!!"

"What do you mean Carol?"

"She had it custom made Beth it is solid gold and has her initials monogrammed on it!!"

"You've got to be kidding Carol!" "No, Beth I am not, I wish I was." 'That is sick Carol!!

"I know Beth, I know." "Where is it Carol?"

"She has it padlocked to the floor under her bed, Beth."

"How can she use it then, Carol?"

"She has it attached to a long chain, so you can pull it out from under the bed and place it under her, Beth!"

"Oh, for God sake Carol"

"It gets worse Beth."

"I am afraid to ask Carol."

"See that life size statue of Lawrence Welk next to her bed, Beth?"

"Yea Carol, I see it."

"Well open his hand Beth and you will see a combination lock."

"Ok Carol I see it."

"Now press 666 Beth, do you hear a click?' "Yea, I hear it Carol."

"That means it's open now Beth, you can push the statue aside, it's not heavy at all."

"Ok, I did it Carol." "What do you see Beth?"

"Oh My God Beth, it is a little hopper to clean bed pans and urinals."

"Yep, Carol, Mrs. Johnlove, has her own hopper exclusively for her bed pan!!"

"Oh my God Beth"

"Get a load this Carol she uses only mountain spring water shipped in from the Colorado Rockies."

"Why Beth?

"She says her bed pan deserves only the best Carol, and that mountain water will make it last for all eternity."

"What a nut job Beth." "You got it Carol."

"What if I slipped a plastic bed pan under Beth?"

"She'd know Carol, she says her ass is specifically designed to recognize her bed pan, and if it's not her bed pan, she will have a severe allergic reaction!"

"That is creepy and nuts Beth!"

"I know, anyway, we are wasting precious time Carol, of which we have none to spare. It's a good thing that an old person's metabolism is so slow, that it takes forever for them

to burn. Quick stick the bed pan under her and maybe s.
will pee and go stinky and we can use the urine to douse the
flames. I'll go out and round up all the old men, they always
have to pee. We'll get them to pee on Mrs. Puff, and that will
put the fire out!"

"Great idea Carol, keep the door open just a crack so we can
still communicate and open all windows so the smoke won't go
in the hallway."

"We don't need a code brown called and the whole place
alarmed, Beth!"

"Carol, isn't code brown, when an old person soils there
depends?"

"No Beth, code brown is a fire, if they yelled fire the geezers
would all panic, they say code brown, so the employees know
what's going on and the deadbeats can do what they do best,
remain clueless."

"Ok Carol, now I understand."

Mrs. Johnlove finally sees her burning roommate and is
terrified by the sight, "Oh my God, I can't stand seeing that
poor woman suffer, pull my curtain shut."

"Shit, wouldn't you know it, any other time you can't get
away from an old man who has to pee, now, when you really
need one, they are nowhere to be found. Wait a minute Beth,
here comes a whole flock of them. They just got back from
"Old Country Buffet". That means they just had there geritol
and milk of magnesia. They should be ready to pee up a storm.

None of them are in a wheel chair so they are all ready to
pee, into action. You who boys, come on over here we've got
something for you."

"What's that you say honey? My hearing aid only picks up
AM not FM."

"Wow that's a shocker, a nutbag answer from a nutbag!"
"What did you say sweetie"

"God Damit will you old fucks get over here, this lady is going to burn to a crisp and President Dee Dee is going to find out if you don't hurry up."

"Ok honey we are coming as fast as we can, we're not spring chickens you know."

"No shit Hurry Up."

"Finally, you dead beats made it here, any longer and we would have been singing camp fire songs and roasting marshmallows over Mrs. Puff."

"I hate marshmallows sweetie they make my dentures stick together and I can't spit at the CNA's, all I can do then is punch and bite, and that is not as fun."

"Oh, shut up Ned, now you boys drop your drawers and diapers and start peeing!"

"Wait a minute I'm confused here!"

"You are supposed to be confused Ned, you are old and have shit for brains, now start peeing."

"Beth, let me see if I got this straight, any time we don't pee in the toilet you holler at us."

"Yes Ned, that is correct."

"Now you are telling us not to pee in the toilet, but to pee on this woman?"

"Yes, you need to pee on this lady, start speaking "Oldese" to your friends and tell them to pee on Mrs. Puff we need to put this fire out!!"

"Well if that don't beat all, I never will understand this younger generation, they don't make any sense, one minute they are telling you to only pee in the toilet, the next minute they are telling you not to pee in the toilet, but to pee on Mrs. Puff, if that don't beat all. No wonder we old people are confused!"

"Ned this is the last time I am going to tell you, if you and your boys don't start peeing on Mrs. Puff instantly I am confiscating all your Ben Gay!!!"

"Shit, she means business boys' whip it out and sta. peeing!!"

Finally, the boys start peeing and dowse Mr. Puff in pee and put out the flames, not a minute too soon. Mrs. Puff is completely unscathed.

"Look at this Carol."

"What is it Beth?"

The diapers the boys took off are soaked with pee Carol, they have yesterday's date marked on them, and they're on backwards."

"Damn Beth! Second and third shift are lazy!" "I better go get President Dee Dee Carol."

"What are you crazy, why would you do that, Beth?" "Carol, she has to know these residents are being abused, going around in wet diapers for 48 hours and no one bothering to check them."

"Are you crazy Beth? Setting a resident on fire isn't exactly humane treatment, if President Dee Dee sees this she'll have us thrown in jail for elder abuse."

"I never thought of that Carol, you are right." "Now I know you are a nurse Beth."

"Why do you say that Carol"

"Because the only thing dumber than a CNA is a nurse and even a C.N.A isn't dumb enough to get President Dee Dee involved a situation like this."

"You don't have to be so mean Carol." "You're right I'm sorry Beth."

"Ok Carol"

"Damn Beth, I don't believe it." "What Carol."

"It is a miracle Beth!" "What is a miracle Carol?"

"Remember Beth, how we always ridiculed Mrs. Puff for lining her body with tons and tons of Kleenex because everything was so scratchy?"

"Yes, Carol I remember, how does she get all that Kleenex anyway, she can't afford it?"

"She gets it from THE LADY WHO DOES THE LAUNDRY Beth!"

"Oh, Ok Carol"

"To think Beth, we always tried to strip the Kleenex off Mrs. Puff, and she screamed bloody murder."

"Yes Carol, President Dee Dee got so fed up with her, she washed her hands of the whole thing, and allowed her to keep wrapping her body in Kleenex."

"Yea Beth, I remember President Dee Dee saying she could care less about that "old dingbat" and her Kleenex."

"So what Carol?"

"You just don't get it do you Beth?" "Get what Carol?"

"AAhh Beth, I give up with you." "Why, what did I do Carol?"

"Mrs. Puff is completely unharmed Beth, only her hair got burnt. She had so many layers of Kleenex covering her body the fire never reached her skin."

"Oh. Now I get it Carol.

"Duh Beth, and all it took was a simple clubbing over the head. Anyway, we can shave her head and tell everyone she became part of some bullshit religious cult or something."

"Won't Mrs. Puff wonder why she is bald Carol?"

"Shit Beth, she is so demented she didn't even know she was on fire, she'll believe us if we tell her she shaved her own head."

"Well Carol, the first time I saw her I swore she was a man, the way she looks and all, I suppose she can't look stranger than any other man with a bald head."

"Of course, not Beth, now you are catching on, that a girl."

Thank you Carol "You're welcome, Beth."

"You done good boys you saved Mrs. Puff's life a prevented FeudalCare from burning to the ground, you boy are heroes."

"Does that mean me and the boys get to keep our Ben Gay".

"It sure does!" "YEEEHAAA!!"

"Here Ned, let me help you pull up your pants."

"Hey, watch what you are doing Beth, those things down there are not meant to be played with!"

"Girls, now that all the fuss is over, can you get me off the bed pan, I've been on it so long I feel like I am married to it." "Mrs. Johnlove, you didn't do anything in the bed pan." "Oh well, false alarm, I guess I did not have to go stinky after all."

CHAPTER 14

Spit Shine and Polish Mrs. Puff

Mrs. Puff thought someone was smoking marijuana outside her bedroom window. When told it was just a dream she was satisfied and did not give it another thought. Thank God her allergy free air filter left not a trace of the mishap in a very short time! Still, she smelled of smoke and needed a bath to cover up the evidence.

"I took a bath 5 years ago I don't need another one." "Quiet Mrs. Puff it is your bath day and you are taking one regardless of what you say. Besides, you have some wax build up in your ear canal that needs to be washed out."

"I've never been on the Erie Canal I don't even know how to swim." "Beth" "Yes Carol"

"This isn't the overnight shift, where you can pull up a chair, sit down, and read the newspaper. On the 3p-11p shift we actually work. Put the paper down, and put that chair away. Use the sit- to- stand lift to get Mrs. Puff up, undressed and into her wheel chair."

"I can't wheel her to the shower room naked Carol."

"Of course, not Beth, nobody wants to see that gross disgusting body unclothed." "What do I do then Carol?"

"Throw a bath blanket over her Beth, there might be kids in the hallway we don't want to scar them for life."

"Of course, not Carol, I am going to splash a ton of cologne on her, so she does not stink up the hall with shit, piss, and smoke."

"Are you crazy Beth? You can't do that." "Why not Carol?"

"Because old people can marinate in shit and piss all day with no adverse effects, Beth. But, the minute perfume and cologne touch their skin, they become violently ill. All old people are allergic to perfume and cologne."

"I did not know that Carol."

"It is a well-known scientific fact Beth, look it up in the Enquirer!"

"I will Carol, thank you very much."

"No problem Beth."

While Beth was getting Mrs. Puff ready Carol went and started her bath water. Suddenly from down the hall she hears screams coming from Mrs. Puff's room. She races down there, enters the room and quickly locks the door. Turns out Mrs. Puff can't even use the sit- to- stand lift, and to make matters worse Beth did not know how to use it properly. She is screaming in agony, with her right leg lifted clear over her head, her left arm hyper-extended over her head, her paralyzed right arm turning blue, and a right foot which is rapidly losing all traction (footing) about to cave in!!

"Oh, shit Beth, quick stuff this sock in her mouth to shut her up, I will lower her back into the bed."

They shut up Mrs. Puff, and put her in her wheel chair. They take her down the hall for her bath. Both Carol and Beth take extra precautions not to walk through the small pox and shingles section of the hall. Accidentally they ram Mrs. Puff's t into a corner of the wall. They are not too concerned about that though, Mrs. Puff can't scream because the sock is in her mouth. The blood they can wash off in the bath tub, and she doesn't need that foot anyway, she has another one.

Wouldn't you know it, Mrs. Puff falls out of her wheel chair, so they have to pick her up and put her back in. Thank God all the other nurses are outside smoking otherwise they'd be totally busted.

Upon entering the bathroom another crisis is in progress, the tub is overflowing and they are ankle deep in water and bubble bath. After what seems like forever, they finally get the mess cleared up and get Mrs. Puff in the tub. Just then the phone rings, since everyone is outside smoking Carol leaves to answer the phone.

"FeudalCare, where we use our catheters on a maximum of only three people may I help you."

"AHHH hi this is the deliveryman I have a large garbage pizza for a Dee Dee Kuntz."

"Beth, can you get the door it's the Pizza guy, lard ass Dee Dee is hungry again."

Beth runs to answer the door and forgets all about poor Mrs. Puff. Several hours later when they get back in there, it's too late Mrs. Puff is dead!! To make matters worse she wasn't wearing her hipsters (underwear with egg cartons sewn in the sides, used for fall protection and floatation).

There is a bright side of this whole fiasco, Mrs. Puffs dreadful suffering filled life is over and Carol and Beth avoided the death penalty. They had to serve life in prison for involuntary manslaughter.

CHAPTER 15
Even Deadbeats Need Appropriate Care

President Dee Dee was simply overwhelmed with the depth and breadth of her responsibilities as President of FeudalCare. As much as she hungered and thirsted to fill her insatiable appetite for power and control, she finally had to admit she could not do it all. She hired Sergeant Annabelle Stinks to oversee appropriate resident care, Stinks being a master at pseudo-love was perfect for the position.

To the ill-informed masses Stinks appeared loving. In reality the only pleasure Stinks took in her miserable existence was to humiliate and belittle. Rather than help, teach, and inspire Stinks always had an axe to grind! She needed to make herself look good at someone else's expense.

It did not take long for Stinks to infect FeudalCare with her gloomy presence. Stinks was a 38-year veteran of the nursing profession. Sergeant Stinks was so inept, her enlistment in the U.S. Army during the Vietnam War, greatly aided the North Vietnamese.

After the war, Stinks began to wreak havoc at hospitals and nursing schools throughout the fruited plain with her toxic

...nor. At FeudalCare, she definitely found a home teaming ...with President Dee Dee. Stinks never did any "real work" ...e just roamed the halls looking for trouble. Unfortunately for her, and fortunately for the Aides, she was always "a day I' late and a dollar short."

Stinks, like President Dee Dee, was the kind of woman who would smoke pot in her house, and call the cops on her neighbors for playing poker in theirs, and not think twice about it. Stinks was the ultimate hypocrite, "do as I say, not as I do." If you "sucked up" to Stinks, you could go home, even if you were perfectly well. If you did not "kiss her ass," you would be forced to work with "one foot in the grave."

"Excuse me ma'am, what is your name," Stinks blurted out in a gravelly voice that could only be achieved by years of chain smoking. The voice was accompanied by a face with the look and texture of a wet worn out catchers' mitt that was left in the sun to dry.

"My name is Zoey, ma'am."

"Hello Zoey my name is Sergeant Annabelle Stinks. President Dee Dee just hired me as the new Procedures Coordinator and this is my first day on the job."

"Pleased to meet you ma'am"

"Likewise, Zoey, what is your position here at FeudalCare?" "I am a Certified Nursing Assistant."

"Well you sure could have fooled me." (Stinks was about to rip Zoey a new asshole for not wearing her name tag)

"What do you mean Ms. Stinks?"

"It is Sergeant Stinks to you I am a veteran of the United States Army. I was overseas fighting for your freedom while punks like you were still in diapers waiting to grow up to bad rap God and your country."

Zoey's looks were deceiving. She looked like a young, naive, girl innocent to the ways of the world. In short, she looked very

gullible. On paper, it looked like Stinks would totally de
Zoey.

Such was not the case. There was no cheese cake in Zoey
The product of a physically and verbally abusive father and an
overbearing mother, Zoey left home at age 15. Having to grow
up in a hurry forced Zoey to develop her coping and defense
skills to a level most middle age adults never attain.

Least you get the wrong idea about Zoey, she was not a
confrontational, hothead, know it all. She was an excellent
worker. If a resident was mad and peed the bed on purpose,
she would never tell another nurse or CNA that a resident was
dry (nudge, nudge, wink, wink, fingers crossed behind the back,
if you know what I mean).

Zoey was a voracious reader who had her sights set on
a career as computer software developer. She was greatly
influenced by two books in particular, The Way of Zen by
Alan Watts, and How to Win Friends and Influence People by
Dale Carnegie. Unlike the self-righteous, sanctimonious, holier
than thou, hypocritical Stinks, who worshipped at the altar of
venture capitalists, corporate raiders, and bible thumpers. Zoey
was much more at home with the Dali Lama's teachings. Zoey
loved teaching new skills to others and genuinely wanted them
to learn, as opposed to Stinks, who merely wanted to rub your
nose in the dirt.

So, if Sergeant Stinks thought she was up against a
"pushover" she had another thing coming! Zoey knew just how
to diffuse the mean, bitter and hateful Annabelle Stinks.

"You are right Sergeant, I owe you a great deal of gratitude
for serving our country. It is not the sunshine patriot, author
or protester, that I owe my freedom. It is you, a Veteran of our
proud military!!"

Talk about being taken back. Stinks nearly lived up to her
name sake and shit in her pants!

Well, ahhh, ahhh, that is right Zoey and, and don't, you get it."

"Not a chance of that ever-happening Sergeant" "Well good, good, ahh, ahh, very, very good"

"Now, what was it you were saying Sergeant Stinks?" "Ahhh, ahhh, yes Zoey, please wear your name tag from now on, I'd like for all our residents and staff to know the owner of that pretty face and smile."

"Yes Sergeant, you are right. I am usually very conscientious about wearing my name tag. I was having car trouble this morning and feared being late for work. So, I raced out of the house, and it wasn't till after I dropped my car off at the shop and walked to work, that I realized I left it on the dashboard. I can run back to the shop and get it on my lunch break?"

"Nonsense dear you don't have to go through all that trouble. I understand your situation completely and I am sure it will never happen again."

"Never ma'am, I mean Sergeant Stinks."

"Well, we both have work that needs to be done Zoey, so have a great day."

"You to Sergeant thank you." "Thank you"

Unbeknownst to both Sergeant Stinks and Zoey, Brittney was on the other side of the partition, and heard the whole episode. She was just coming off her 15 minutes of work and was now ready for a long overdue break.

"Hi Brittney, how are you?"

"Fine Zoey, who was that BITCH"

"Sergeant Stinks, President Dee Dee just hired her today." "For what"

"Get a load of this bull shit Brittney, her title is Procedures Coordinator."

"Oh, for God Sake, another Henchman"

"Ya"

"I heard the whole thing Zoey, I just got back from Ad Dixons room she set her alarm clock so she would not miss he sleeping pill."

"Is she the lady who sounds like a cat meowing when she talks Brit?"

"No Zoey that is Haley Tosis, Addy looks like Beetlejuice, from her years of abusing Darvocet and Ativan. Addy Dixon is the one who I thought was a goat from the petting zoo, the first time I heard her, but could not see her face. It sounds like she is saying baaa baaa baaa but is actually saying, "I love you with all my heart."

"Wow! That is freaky Brit!" "Yea it is Zoey.

"Anyway, Britt, Stinks is off on another witch hunt now." "Well, you handled that great Zoey, I would have freaked if she started her inquisition on me."

"Just tell her what wants to hear Brittney, and you'll be fine, hold still Brit."

"I am not going to refill anything Zoey, what are you talking about?"

"I said hold still Britt, not what are you going to refill. You have an empty syringe sticking out of your back pocket." "Oh, thank you Zoey, that is dangerous, I need to be more careful."

"I'll say, but think nothing of Brit, just looking out for you.".

"Thanks Zoey, I appreciate that." "No problem Brit."

"It is really a shame Zoey, a lot of good people wind up leaving the healthcare field, because some nurse is more interested in gratifying their own ego, than wanting others to learn."

"The constant backstabbing and witch hunts, take its toll Brittney. It is much easier to work in an environment where people look out for you, as opposed to healthcare, where they want to "nail your ass to the wall.""

"Thank you for your advice Zoey." "You are welcome."

"Shit"

"What is it Britt?"

"I just forgot I was going to go out "partying" with a friend from high school tonight."

"What is the problem with that Brittney?" "Well, Mrs. Croaker is about to die."

"I know Britt, but we all have to go sometime."

"No Zoey, I don't give a shit about that, it's just if she dies I have to clean up the body for the undertaker, and I will be late getting to the bar. They better give her more "phine" instead of les "phine", so she hurries up and dies early in the shift!"

"We could give her a "morphsicle," Brit." "What is that Zoey?"

"It is a popsicle made out of frozen morphine, Brit." "Ha Ha Ha that is a good one Zoey"

"We could put her on input and outputs, fluid restriction, daily weights, vital signs, run some labs, give her eye drops and coat her body with savvy, and she'll live forever, Brit."

"Another very funny one Zoey, you are on a roll today!! Seriously though, I don't want her to live forever, just long enough for me to go party tonight."

"An emergency tracheotomy is foolproof Brit, it either kills them right away, or prolongs there life for another twenty four hours, either way, you a free and clear to hit the bars."

"I hope I get to go Zoey."

"Brittney, I think you are worrying for no reason. Mrs. Croaker is a very considerate, she will die for you early in the shift, then, you will be able to clean her up and still be able to hit the "partying scene" with plenty of time to spare."

"Oh Zoey, do you think so? I hope you are right." Yea, I am positive, Brit.

"Thank goodness Zoey, that is a load off my mind. I tried calling about a dozen CNA's to work for me, but no one answered the phone."

"That's probably because they are already on their way to work for you Brit."

"Yea that's it Zoey!"

Meanwhile, back at the ranch. Stinks is roaming the halls looking for trouble She accidentally set down a double helping of pills on the counter top that Old Lady Jenkins chugged down. Oh well, I am sure they were for her anyway. Besides, Stinks really needed a cigarette, so it is ok.

Ellie just found some toothpaste. She only has six of teeth, but would still like to keep them clean. She thought of leaving a chunk of toothpaste in her mouth and accusing an aide of toothpaste abuse but decided against it.

It is very difficult to tell why a senior citizen acts goofy. Research has narrowed it down to three possibilities, a urinary tract infection, venereal disease from a bad patch of diapers, or eating paint chips as a baby.

CHAPTER 16

Wide Load

Stinks is back from her smoke and instructs a volunteer to take the residents back to their respective rooms. Stink loves volunteers, unlike other employees, they earn their pay.

Suddenly Stinks hears a sound in another part of the building, a sound she has not heard the likes of since her days in Nam, when a detonating bomb, was an everyday occurrence. Fights break out all the time when two or more old geezers call bingo at the same time. They bash each other's' skulls in with their canes, but this noise is way too loud for that.

After checking it out, much to Stinks chagrin, there is no disaster. It is just Althea "Big Mama" Jertsen heading to the snack machine. "Big Mamma's weight is within defined limits, four hundred pounds, down from six hundred, three months ago, after having a two-hundred-pound tumor liposuctioned out of her. She insists it was an excess of cheese sandwiches.

Daily "Big Mamma" emerges from her room about this time to hit the twinkie's in the vending machine! She is a severe diabetic, so every day the nurses make sure they pump her fat ass full of insulin before she goes out to rummage. Some anal-retentive nurse's worry about pissing off her doctor, but most don't give a damn.

This is an everyday occurrence, but this being Stinks' day on the job she almost did her namesake once again. T reason for the apparent earthquake is twofold. One being "Big Mamma's" girth and the second and of equal importance is her shaking and unsteady gait. When her trembling hands hit the walker and the walker pounds into the ground with the force of an electric jackhammer, pits and pieces of the concrete floor shatter, and go flying. Surprisingly her balance is not that bad, on the rare occasion that she does fall, she never gets hurt! She has way too much blubber to break a "HIPPA".

CNA's have likened getting her up to lifting a Volkswagen. She is too much work to get up the conventional way. CNA's have been fired for leaving her in bed during meals. Their reasoning that she is fat enough and does not need to eat did not go over with the late Dewey Screwem and Ann Howe. President Dee Dee is of like mind and refused to hire the ex FeudalCare CNA's back when she took the helm.

An alternative more moderate approach, to restrict her to a 1000 calorie a day, dubbed operation "Chunk on the Trunk Removal," was a miserable failure. She continually hallucinated, calling out for Big Mac's and pork rinds, keeping everyone awake at night.

CHAPTER 17

Recreation

Ironically "Big Mamma" and her roommate are the only residents to have bunk beds. Naturally "Big Mamma's" family insisted she take the top bunk. Her family does not really like her and they are hoping FeudalCare really messes up and kills or at least injures her, so they can sue and collect on a big law suit.

"Big Mamma" thinks she is in the top bunk, so if she dies it won't be so hard for God to lift her up to heaven. There is no problem with her falling. Her considerable girth protects her bones, and now that the trampoline has been strategically placed she ricochet's off the floor and right back into bed.

For shits and grins CNA's push her off the top bunk. It is a lot easier to plop her on the floor and let her bounce to bed, than it is to lift her up the bunk bed steps. The late Screwem and Howe, I am sure are turning over in their graves (after laughing their ass oft).

The Gestapo (State Inspectors) would love to catch them in the act. First off because off the record, they would find it hilarious too, but most importantly so they could be righteously indignant, sanctimonious, and impose a huge fine on FeudalCare. It would be a great opportunity for them to line their pockets.

President Dee Dee would be beside herself and Serge Stinks would be delirious with joy, if she caught them in the ac It would validate the importance of her job, and of course make her feel, holier than thou.

Entertainment in the elder care industry it is imperative. Hockey was suggested by one of the new CNA's. While an interesting idea it was shot down for a number of reasons. Obviously, the CNA was not aware of the ban on sporting events imposed at FeudalCare some time ago. It would cost a fortune to replace broken dentures every time an old foggie got checked into the boards and they went flying out of their mouth. Seniors falls happen left and right even under the best of conditions, on ice skates it would be an utter disaster, a never-ending cycle of broken bones and vital signs.

Playing super ball with Big Mamma was a source of amusement CNA's could get away with, but it is not the only one. If you really want to piss off old demented man, perform range of motion (rom) exercises on their welded shut joints. I can guarantee you will learn a whole new vocabulary of cuss words. Perfectly set up under the guise of physical therapy you can aggravate the shit out of an old man and there is not a damn thing Sergeant Stinks or anyone else can do about it. They are merely abiding by the residents "plan of care." What right minded person would not want a resident to derive maximum benefits from their care plan!

If you thought bumper cars at the amusement park were fun, you haven't seen anything yet. Try putting ten old geezers in a room with only their walkers and wheelchairs. They will knock each other over so quickly, it will make the action on a pinball wizard's machine look like slow motion. Boy I tell you, C.N.A shave got to be the biggest scumbags on the face of the earth to treat our old people like this, next to nurses that is.

CHAPTER 18

Its Payback Time Boys!!

Throughout history, it has been a male dominated world. Whether business, finance, law, even cooking, fat old rich white men have ruled the roost. It is not fair or just, but that is just the way it has been. Hell, women were not even allowed to vote in the USA until 1920. It was not all that long ago, that the husband was the "breadwinner" and went off to work while the wife stayed home, cared for the children, cooked and cleaned.

Nursing was one of the rare exceptions to this rule. It was, and still is a predominantly woman dominated field. Men have started to make some inroads into the profession in the 21^t century, as women have done in business, law and finance. However, nursing is their baby, and they are not going to give it up without a fight. This is especially true amongst the dinosaurs in the profession. When Shakespeare said, "hell hath no fury like a woman's scorn" he obviously was referring to old women in the nursing profession.

Don't get me wrong, men are just as big of assholes as women, if not more so, it's just that they are assholes in a different way. Men are more violent than women if they are pissed at one another they will pick up a wet floor sign and nail you over the head, or plow you over with a food cart. When comes to pettiness though, women have cornered the market!

Ed a 23-year-old rookie nurse, who just passed the boards, was in for the shock of his life.

"Hello Edward my name is Rhonda and I will be your trainer for the next month. Getting you familiar with FeudalCare and prepared to perform your job-related tasks".

"Your hair is really cute, Rhonda!"

"What is that supposed to mean Edward? Are you implying that my hair was ugly yesterday?"

"Not at all Rhonda, I was not even here yesterday." "Then are you coming on to me?"

"No Rhonda I was not coming on to you, I was just ahhh, ahhh!"

"Oh, I see Edward I am not attractive enough for you to ask out, is that right?"

"No Rhonda, you are very attractive, that is not the case at all."

"Then skip the preliminaries and get to the main event, you were coming on to me, you were going to ask me out?"

"No, I mean yes, I mean no, yes, no, oh, I don't know what I mean!"

"If I was a man Edward, would you have complimented me on my hair?"

"Well, no"

"Why not"

"Well, ahhh, ahhh, I don't know, I suppose people would think I was a little peculiar, if! said a man's hair was cute!"

"Oh, so you think gay people are peculiar is that right Edward!"

"No Rhonda, not at all."

"Good, because I have a gay male friend who always compliments me on my hair and clothes, you are not gay are **you?**"

"No, not at all, I am married actually and have 2 children!" "Well, that does not mean you can't be gay."

"I realize that Rhonda but I am not gay." "What's wrong with being gay?"

"There is nothing wrong with being gay Rhonda, nothing at all."

"You know Edward, since you are married, you should not be complimenting other women's hair."

"Rhonda, you have got me so confused and worried. This happens to me every time I am around females, I try to be nice and complimentary and wind up doing everything wrong!"

"That is ridiculous Edward, you are being paranoid, maybe you need to see a psychologist!"

"I don't need a psychologist Rhonda, what I need for you to do is stop exacerbating my problem. What I need is some compassion from you."

"Edward, there is no room in the nursing profession for compassion!"

"Rhonda, it is hard being a new nurse, trying to perform task you are not familiar with and on top of that having to worry about you telling President Dee Dee and Sergeant Stinks, that I sexually harassed you."

"Boy Edward, you sure are touchy whatever gave you the idea I was that type of person who would run and yell sexual harassment?"

"I don't know paranoia I guess." "Edward".

"Yes Rhonda"

"I am glad you like my hair"

"Good, I am glad."

"And, don't worry I am not going to run and tattle tale President Dee Dee or Sergeant Stinks. At least while she is eating any way!"

"Oh no"

"It's a joke Edward, I am kidding" "Good, that is a relief."

"OK let's get started then."

"'Great!"

'The most important thing in any nursing home is paperwork. Paperwork is the life blood of healthcare. Without paperwork, the industry would be completely paralyzed and have to shut down, it simply could not function."

"That really sucks Rhonda, I wasn't even going to do paperwork at all, I was just going to leave everything blank." "Oh my God Edward, don't even say that, not even in jest!"

"I chart by exception Rhonda, if there is no charting there is no exception, and if there no exception, there is no charting, then I am free and clear!"

"Well, you can't do that Edward, paperwork is the most important thing in nursing!"

"I thought caring for patients was the most important thing in nursing Rhonda."

"Yea right Edward, if you don't chart, your ass is going to get sued."

"If you take good care of patients you won't get sued Rhonda."

"Sure Edward, Santa Claus is real, if you go to college, work hard, and be good, you will make a lot of money. Anyway, the most important form is right here. It is the paperwork confirming you did the paperwork on the paperwork you voided."

"What?"

"Oh, never mind Edward, you will catch on." "Rhonda there is a light on."

"Oh, that is Mr. Model. He is the sweetest thing. I am the ONLY one he will let take care of him. The other nurses and aides think he can't talk, but that is only because he does not like them. He talks to me all the time. He said, I love you Rhonda, I was so happy, I shed a tear."

"What does Mr. Model do when you are not here Rhonda?"

"Oh, I don't know, ROTS I guess, let's get back to your training."

"Shouldn't someone answer his light?"

"No, he is just a dirty old man who is too lazy to get up and go to the bathroom so he calls for his urinal or the bad pan."

"I still think we should check it out Rhonda, it may be something serious."

"Boy Edward, you have a lot to learn about nursing, trust me, a nurse never answers a call light or a plea for help that is what those low life CNA's are for!

"What do I do then Rhonda?" "One of two things, Edward" "I am listening Rhonda"

"You pretend you don't see or hear the problem Edward. President Dee Dee is a real pro at that. If you feel guilty about doing that, track down a CNA to get the call light."

"I think that is terrible Rhonda."

"As long as you remember the cardinal rule of nursing, you will be fine Edward."

"What's that?"

"If it looks important it is not. And, if it looks trivial, it is important! Remember that Edward, and you can be a nurse forever."

"That does not sound right Rhonda." "Trust me Edward, all nurses do it."

"Well, I suppose Rhonda you're the teacher, if you say so it must be true."

"That is the spirit Edward, now you are catching on." "Thanks Rhonda."

"Don't mention it Edward."

Just when it looked like Rhonda and Edward were making some headway, Rhonda was stricken with a severe case of gas, cramps, and ovarian pain and had to go home. Nurse Richard had to fill in. By no means was Richard able to fill Rhonda's shoes, but he was serviceable and capable of getting Rhonda out of Edward's heart!

While Edward was waiting for Richard to clock in, get a cup of coffee, and popcorn, he kept himself busy by observing some of the other nurses at work. He observed one nurse whose face screamed twenty-five years of utter hell. She was cursing of all things about eye drops. A resident kept her eyes slammed shut, so she could not administer them. Another residents eye drops were no were to be found, even after frantically searching the medicine cart, and turning it upside down.

What the hell is she getting all upset about eye drops for Edward thought, maybe she knows something I don't but what the fuck does it matter if a ninety-three-year-old decrepit person does not get their eye drops! It is not as if it is going to destroy the quality of their life. Just mark down you gave them and move on. If anyone questions her, all she has to say is "they were there when I gave them I don't know what could have happened to them."

In addition to being petty Edward was beginning to get the impression a lot of nurses are a couple of bacon strips short of a grand slam. No matter how much you try to help an old person, when they scream in agony, you always think it is your fault but it isn't. You are damned if you do, and damned if you don't, when dealing with the elderly. How could nurses not see that, especially veteran nurses? Richard is ready to go, so it's time for Edward to get down to business.

"Hello Edward, my name is Richard I will be filling in for the vacationing Rhonda."

"Nice to meet you Richard" "Likewise, Edward"

"I don't know how much orientation Rhonda was able to give you?"

"We just started the first topic we broached was paperwork." "Ahhh paperwork the life blood of our industry."

'That is what Rhonda said, I still can't believe that, I though caring and compassion was the life blood of the industry."

"Oh Edward, I can see I have a lot of work to do with you. How old are you Edward?"

"I am 22 and just graduated from Liver Sea School of Nursing with a BSN. Why do you ask?"

"Just curious, I was all wide eyed, bushy tailed and ready to save the world, when I graduated nursing school as well. But alas, that was years ago. I thought if you graduated college, worked hard, and were a good person, you were set for life."

"What happened to you Richard?"

"A thing called reality slapped me in the face."

In a utopia, compassion and caring are what it is all about. But, we don't live in a perfect world, we work at FeudalCare, and at FeudalCare, the name of the game is survival. If you can put in an eight-hour work day, and not get fired, sued, or thrown in jail, you've had a great day.

CHAPTER 19

It's Chow Time

"Let's start your orientation with something grounded in reality, food."

"Why food Richard"

"Because it is lunch time all the residents and staff are in the doing room. I know what you are thinking Edward I am a nurse I did not go to college for 4 years to pass food trays. Well that is not the way it is every nurse passes trays at FeudalCare. Anyway, food is simple, everybody loves it, and you need it to survive. Outside of sleep, going to the bathroom, and taking pain pills, food is all an old person has!"

"Ok Richard, I have no problem passing trays, I don't look upon it as being beneath me, I am all for anything I can do to help out!!"

Edward and Richard chat, as they pass trays, pour beverages and clean up.

"Suppose you only have two pieces of bread left Edward, one fresh and the other stale, and there are two residents that want bread, what do you do?"

"I don't know Richard."

"Well if one of them is demented, you give him the stale piece Edward."

"Why Richard"

"He won't know the difference Edward." "That sounds mean Richard."

"It may sound mean Edward, but it is the real world." "What if they are both alert Richard?"

"Good question Edward. You give the fresh bread to the one you like, and the stale bread to the one you don't like!"

"That does not sound right Richard."

"Edward, what I am giving you is reality-based nursing training. Good solid practical life nursing. None of that text book theory nonsense."

"I don't know Richard."

"Trust me Edward, some day you will thank me for this. This is real life nursing." "I suppose so Richard."

"You will see the light eventually Edward. Let me ask you another question."

"OK Richard."

"You are in the dining room, Edward, and a hamburger falls off the tray and on to the floor, what do you do?"

"Get a broom and dust pan and sweep it up Richard?" "No, no, no, Edward that takes too long. By the time you find a dust pan and sweep it up, a hundred residents could be in distress because you took your eye off them."

"What do I do then Richard?"

"You have the decency and the common courtesy to kick it under the counter."

"Are you serious Richard?" "Serious as a heart attack Edward"

"Are heart attacks contagious Richard?"

"I don't think so Edward, as long as you wear gloves." "So it is OK for a non-heart attack person to room with a heart attack person Richard?"

"As long as you keep the curtain between the two be separate so the heart attack germs can't spread."

"Cool Richard thank you." "No problem Edward."

"Anyway, getting back to the subject, yes, I am serious you kick the burger under the counter Edward."

"Wow Richard, nursing sure is not what I thought it would be."

"Nothing ever is Edward, but at-least now, you are learning."

Lunch is now over, so Richard and Edward begin to escort residents back to their rooms and Richard continues his instruction.

CHAPTER 20
The Necessary Room

"Let's move on to toileting Edward. It is a scientifically proven fact that a senior citizen spends ninety eight percent of their life on the toilet, thinking about going to the toilet, or wishing they could go to the toilet."

"WOW Richard, that is amazing."

"I bet they don't teach you important stuff like that in nursing school Edward."

"No, they sure don't Richard."

"Kind of figured that Edward, anything relevant they skip right over. Why just the other day an aide came running to me crying that Mr. Merriweather had been abused. I asked her how. In between tears and sobs, wanting so and so to be fired, calling the state etc., she finally blurted out that he had been left on the toilet for six hours and had fallen asleep."

"Oh, I thought you were going to say a resident was abused because someone ran over their foot with a wheelchair Richard."

"No Edward, that isn't abuse!" "Why not Richard"

"Because Edward, they have another foot anyway. Usually when a resident yell that their foot was room over by a wheelchair, the wheelchair did not come within twelve inches of their foot."

"Oh, I see. Hey Richard" "Yes Edward"

"What is the worlds' record for someone sitting on the toilet Richard."

"Good question Edward, I don't know."

"That's OK, Richard. I will look it up in the Guinness Book of World records. Sorry go ahead and continue."

"Thank you, she thought I was going to be all upset and rant and rave. She was quite disappointed when I wasn't." "What did you do Richard?"

"I went and told President Dee Dee Edward." "You mean you ratted someone out Richard?"

"No, Edward of course not, I would never do that, I wanted to patent the idea of "toilet dwelling", intentionally leaving residents on the toilet. And, I wanted a raise for coming up with the idea!"

"What! A perplexed Edward replies."

"Think about it Edward, how many times has an old geezer walked around in a wet and dirty diaper that weighs forty pounds?"

"Quite a lot Richard"

"Edward, since seniors spend 98% of their life going to the bathroom, or thinking about going to the bathroom, the cost saving will be astronomical."

"I don't follow you Richard."

"Ok, Edward, look at it this way. We sit a senior on the toilet and give him a sleeping pill. He does not know where he is anyway, so he can live his whole life on the toilet. We no longer need beds, diapers, clothing etc. He can have all the conveniences of modem day living and live a full and productive life, right from the comfort and luxury of his own toilet!"

"What about skin break down and toilet sores from sitting in the same spot all the time Richard?"

"Good question Edward. I am way ahead of you. Every two hours we hoist them up on the sit- to- stand lift, and slap some bacon grease on their ass and plop them back down."

"Hmmm, it might work Richard."

"Might? Why this is going to revolutionize the geriatric care industry."

"Good luck Richard, I wish you well, and hope it works out for you."

"Thank you, Edward, it will. You are so lucky to have me as a trainer."

How come?

"Well Edward, it is like this. It took me a lifetime to realize that everything they teach you growing up is a lot of bullshit."

"How so Richard"

"Well Edward, let's look at a couple of the myths you are brainwashed into believing growing up. My all-time favorite, watch me blow this one to smithereens!"

"Go ahead Richard, I am ready."

"Everything happens for a reason Edward. What a load of shit that is. There is no reason either of us should be born in the USA, with more than enough food to eat, while other human beings are born in countries where they starve to death."

"Interesting point Richard, I never thought of it that way."

"Things happen because they do Edward, not because of any divine plan. If you throw one hundred marbles up in the air why do some land under the coffee table, others in the middle of the floor, and others under the sofa?" "I have no idea Richard, why?"

"Because they do Edward, another good one is if you be good everything will be Ok. That's a load of crap! I followed my parents and societies rules completely, made no deviations from them, and I suffered from a case of depression so bad, it is a wonder I am still alive today to talk about it."

"I am sorry to hear that Richard, this is not the kind of stuff you hear every day in training!"

"Edward, Corporate America doesn't want you to know they are feeding you a line of bullshit. That way they can keep you under their thumb. If people really knew how bad they are getting fucked over, there would be mass revolution on our hands."

"That is true Richard, I never thought of that, any more bits of wisdom?"

"My all-time favorite Edward, is if you work hard, you will be successful."

"That is not true Richard?"

"Of course, not Edward, that is something society brainwashes us with. That way the ten percent of the population who are greedy, lie, obsess about money, are ruthless, exploit people, are selfish, and back stab, can control ninety percent of the wealth!"

"My parents or teachers never taught me that!"

"I know Edward, I know, anyway, let's get back to nursing."
"OK Richard."

"I have a question for you Edward."

"Ok Richard."

"When you are passing medication Edward, what do you think is the most important thing?"

"Whether to serve a single or double helping of pillsRichard?"

"No Edward."

"Insulin, Richard?" "No Edward." "Lasix, Richard"

"No Edward, think remember the cardinal rule of nursing, if it's trivial make it important, and if it's important, make it trivial."

"I give up Richard, what is it?"

"Eye drops and skim- milk, Edward." "What, Richard, I don't follow you."

"Edward, if a person has one foot in the grave, invariably, without fail, a doctor will prescribe eye drops."

"Why Richard"

"Because, they can Edward"

"What do you mean Richard?"

"Doctors love to fuck with nurses Edward!" "Oh, how so Richard"

"By prescribing unnecessary medications Edward, by writing prescriptions that serve no purpose, other than making nurses lives a living hell. Take Jim Milner for example a resident in that room over there."

"He looks like he is fed up with life Richard, he has no longer has any desire to live, he does not do anything for himself."

"Yea that is the guy Edward. He resists and doesn't cooperate with anyone who tries to help him. Well, his doctor prescribes three different eye drops six times a day, for a grand total of eighteen frikin times a day you've to put eye drops in the motherfuckers' eyes!"

"Oh, I can't believe any doctor would do that Richard?" "Sure, Edward and President Dee Dee has an inner beauty!" "What about the skim milk, Richard?"

"Oh yea, Edward, Rosemary the resident in 150 bed 2, she swears skim milk will cure every disease known to man and if she continues to take skim milk, she will live forever."

"What does her Doctor say Richard?"

"He agrees with her Edward, he tells us to give her all her medicine with skim milk, just to shut her up, so she will leave him the hell alone.

"I can't say that I blame him Richard."

"Neither do I Edward, but it will give you an idea how messed up and screwy healthcare is, and nothing is as it seems!"

"Wow! What is that guy over there yelling Richard? Scotch on the Rocks?"

"No, Edward he is yelling scratch my nuts, he has a terrible rash on his testicles."

"Oh, ok Richard"

"And falls, you talk about a nightmare Edward, oh my God, falls suck beyond belief."

"Why Richard, because It is so sad when an elderly person gets hurt"

"Hell, no Edward, I could care less about that. There you go, thinking inside the box again, like a typical nurse, I don't give a shit if these old pieces of crap fall (besides they never get hurt anyway). Every time one of these old fucks butt or knees hit the ground, it as an hour and a half of additional paperwork."

"Kind of takes all the fun out of falling, doesn't it Richard?"

"Yes Edward, residents have a right to fall, until they actually fall, then it is our fault, .and an extra hour and a half of aggravation to boot!"

"Is that a broken electric motor, there is a strange sound coming from maintenance room?"

"No Edward, that is old man Comesperm, the Aides are getting him ready for a bath he hates it so he makes that sound."

"This is sure a strange place, Richard."

"That it is Edward, and you have not even met Marty yet. He is a CNA who is constantly cleaning. He keeps a checklist of everything he does, no one gives a shit about that, but Marty does it!! What a kook!"

"That lady sounds like a goat Richard."

"Yea, it does Edward, she is just saying I love you. She says that to everyone, if she met the Boston Strangler, she would even say it to him. Don't get me wrong Edward, this job is not all misery and doom and gloom, you can make it fun."

"How Richard"

"Well, take for example when you give a shot Edward."
"Like insulin Richard?"

"Yea, Edward, I love to go duck hunting, but since the duck hunting season is so short, and I work so much, I don't get much chance to go. So, I make a game out of giving a shot, and pretend like I am hunting."

"How do you do that Richard?"

"Filling the syringe with insulin is the equivalent offloading pellets into the shot gun. Putting the needle on their fat ass is like aiming at the duck, and pushing the plunger is like pulling the trigger of the gun."

"You have a vivid imagination Richard."

"Thank you, Edward. You have to in this business, if you don't want to go crazy. It certainly takes the boredom out of passing meds and mundane insulin shots, and best of all I bag every target I never miss!"

"That is funny Richard"

"Oh, look Edward it is Albert, one of my favorite residents."
"Hey Richard, I thought Albert was the real fat dude with "man boobs." The guy with the bed sheets stuck between his fat rolls, and the sheets are always dragging on the floor?" "No Edward that is Troy, good morning Albert." "Mourning, I am not mourning Richard, I am fine!" "Albert, you really should wear your ted hose so your legs don't swell up."

"Ted's hose, I never borrowed Ted's hose Richard, I borrowed Ted's sprinkler."

"We have to get back to work Albert. We'll see you later.

Be careful and use your walker, I don't want you to fall."
"Fall, it's not fall yet Richard, the leaves are not changing colors it's still spring."

"Good Bye Albert, see you later."

"See? For Christ sake Richard, I can't see a God Damn thing without my glasses."

"Albert, you are not hearing a thing I am saying, put your hearing aid in."

"Hearing, I ain't got no court hearing!"

CHAPTER 21
Edward Comes of Age

I did not take Edward long to realize what a crock of shit nursing is. It is an industry filled with stupid, self-righteous, sanctimonious, holier than thou hypocrites! Being the father of two and a husband, dropping out of society was not an option. Dealing with the bullshit was going to be like trying to defend LeBron James on the basketball court. You can't stop it all you can do is contain it. As Billy Joel says, "we did not start the fire, it's always been burning since the world has been turning."

Edward decided to make a game of it called "Let's Loosen the Stranglehold." Immediately he felt a sense of relief. When you are braced and prepared for a situation, it is much easier to handle.

The first three months or so, he was very naive and actually believed nursing was about caring, compassion, and making a difference in peoples' lives. He was sadly mistaken! Sure, he felt gratified at first, but the gratification was short lived. It was not long before he realized a compliment does not mean shit when the Gestapo (Department of Public Health), Director of Nursing, or the Administrator, is grilling you on why ninety-nine-year-old deranged Betsy fell, and broke her dilapidated hip. When blame needs to be spread around, a doctor's order not to send a resident to the hospital becomes irrelevant and the nurse becomes the fall guy!

The greatest irony about Nursing is that the actual job is fun. Giving shots, dispensing medication, changing catheters, drawing blood, etc. are challenging and rewarding tasks. It is the "non-nursing" bullshit, the twenty-four hour a day, seven days a week witch hunts, by the likes of President Dee Dee, Sergeant Stinks, the D.O.N., fellow nurses, aides, families, residents, administrators, the state, etc. that make the job a living hell! Ninety-nine great jobs don't mean shit, when one bad job is threatening your livelihood.

CHAPTER 22

Observation Day

Two young nursing students Steve and Harry commence rounds at the FeudalCare nursing home. As they are walking down the hall and huge CLANG echoes throughout the building and Steven stumbles. Turns out a dumb ass nurse left a portable oxygen tank right in the middle of the hall. Steven regains his composure as Harry reads the note attached to the tank.

"Does not put out like it should"

Harry nudges Steven in the ribs. "Hey Steven, this tank is just like your dates!" Steven can take a joke with the best of them after all, he did get into nursing.

As the two resume their walk down the hallway, they are alarmed to see what looks like smoke coming from the shock therapy room. Sure, enough old man Periwinkles' head caught on fire during his shock treatment, and is smoking up a storm. Nothing to worry about though, two social workers put out the fire, but not before roasting a couple of hot dogs.

As they proceed down their walk, they are chastised by an elderly old lady pushing a shopping cart. She obviously is totally demented or she has a urinary tract infection. "I am not your nurse, CNA or house keeper, I am not paying you two boys for it!"

"Must be a former nurse Harry."

"I know Steven see what we have to look forward to." "We should have just stayed behind the counter and looked at charts Harry."

"You are right Steven nothing good can ever come from leaving the nurses' station!"

"Look at this sheet Harry, it is absolutely disgusting. How morbid, how can they get away with this?" "Get away with what Steven?"

"It is a death pool Harry."

"That is revolting Steven! I would like to get some of that action on "Old Lady Turklewicz" though she is getting twenty to one odds to kick the bucket tonight. That is a sure thing."

"Harry, I can't believe you are saying that, you are terrible!"

"Oh, come on Steven it's not like she is being shot down in the prime of life at ninety-eight."

"I guess you're right Harry, the place is jam packed with wall to wall old people. It's not like they are going to miss one or two if someone kicks the bucket.

"Exactly Steven, that reminds me, it's like when one of the old douche bags walks out the door and sounds the alarm."

"I know what you're talking about Harry it is called Code R or something like that."

"Something like that Steven, anyway, I don't see why it is such a big deal that every resident in the building is accounted for. Taking care of these dip shits is not an exact science. As long as you are plus or minus two or three residents it should be OK!"

"Harry, I could not agree with you more. I will go even one better."

"What's that Steven?"

Instead of those damn wander guards, they ought to insert one of those microchips in each resident. They could do it the same time they put their pacemakers in. That way when they escape, the pound could just bring them back on their next dog round up."

"That is both brilliant and hysterical at the same time Steven."

"Much obliged Harry!"

"Look at this Steven, instructions for evacuation in the event of a fire. WOW!!"

"I'll tell you what Harry, in the event of a fire, the only one I'm evacuating is me, these "Golden Oldies" have already lived their life, mine is still ahead of me."

"Bingo again Steven"

Before heading out to check out the action in the dining room, Harry and Steven decide to be polite and ask Grandpa Herb how he's doing.

"How are you doing this morning Grandpa Herb?" "Well, not good boys."

"What's the matter?"

"I am scared to live, because I might get sick and die. I haven't had a bowel movement in six weeks, and I am being poisoned to death by sperm on my leg. I was up all-night peeing because I drank so much coffee, and the worst thing that happened to me is I broke my hand when I went to punch a CNA and he moved, so my hand hit the door knob."

"Yea, yea, yea that is great Grandpa, glad to hear it." "We had to ask Harry."

"I know Steven that is what we get for trying to be polite. I really don't give a damn how he is doing."

"Let's head to the dining room Harry, two p.m. can't come soon enough. I want to get the hell out of here!"

"Steven, would you like some scrambled eggs?"

"No thank you Granny, you eat it Granny, so you grow up to be big and strong."

"*Hi Butt*"

"You better watch it Harry, someone will accuse you of abusing a resident by calling them butt."

"It's a nickname Steven, Her name is Butler, so I shortened **it.**"

"I am telling you Harry you better watch it, If Alexis got fired for forging BM's and urine output, anything is possible."

"I will Steven."

"Don't get me wrong Harry, it's not like you are doing anything terrible like fracturing the bones of elderly people or not mitering their bed sheets, but still you better watch it."

"I will Steven." "Good Harry"

"Hey Steven, did Scwartz get fired for running "Old Lady Jenkins" dentures through the dish washer?"

"They were all set to Harry, but get a load of this. It winds up she loved the scent of Cascade, so finally she was compliant with wearing her dentures, so they kept him around."

"'WOW!'"

"Oh my God Harry look at that shit, the old fucks are having a food fight. Jones just nailed Hickman in the nuts with a hardboiled egg."

"Good thing he does not need those anymore Steven"

"T 11 say Harry."

"Steven, I thought shit like that only happened during bingo?"

"Not anymore Harry."

"That is good news for FeudalCare Steven. Hick man was only scheduled for the short-term vacation package. Now that he has been severely injured he will have to upgrade to the long-term vacation package."

"Harry, this industry is really a death trap. Rule enforcement is so selective and arbitrary."

"In more ways than one Steven"

"Seriously Steven there must be fifty-one ways to leave you lover, I mean get fired."

#1 Preventing a stroke by giving an aspirin, but not having a doctor's order.

#2 Forcing a resident to drink their health shake.

#3 Not forcing a resident to drink their health shake.

#4 Pouring their health shake down the drain.

#5 Leaving a resident to get a towel

#6 Not leaving a resident to get a towel

#7 Two residents falling at the same time

#8 Only stopping one from falling

#9 Not stopping the other

#10 Using a possey restraint

#11 A fall turning into a back flip because of a possey restraint

#12 Feeding a resident

#13 Not feeding a resident

#14 Using too much force to get a resident out of bed

#15 Not using enough force to get a resident out of bed

#16 Using a gait belt

#17 Not using a gait belt

#18 Secretly giving the resident the finger

#19 Secretly telling a resident to shut the fuck up

#20 Not pulling a resident up in bed

#21 Pulling a resident up in bed and having his head hit the head board

#22 Not being nice

#23 Being too nice

#24 Not checking bed alarms

#25 Not using bed alarms

#26 Disconnecting bed alarms

#27 Turning bed alarms off

#28 Taking batteries out of bed alarms

#29 Hiding bed alarms

#30 Throwing bed alarms in trash

#31 Answering a bed alarm two hours later

#32 Combing hair to hard

#33 Not coming hair

#34 Carrying resident like a baby

#35 Not carrying a resident like a baby

#36 Putting someone in isolation

#37 Not putting someone in isolation

#38 Not following HIPPA

#39 Causing someone to break a hip

#40 Calling in sick

#41 Not calling in sick

#42 Telling a fib

#43 Causing a resident to go a-fib

#44 Putting a resident to bed

#45 Not putting a resident to bed.

#46 Letting a resident fall

#47 Not letting a resident fall

#48 Giving a resident a shower

#49 Not giving a resident a shower

#50 Letting a resident stink

#51 Not letting a resident stink

CHAPTER 23

Not Your Dads' Hospice

Back in the day when a person went on hospice, a nurse was with them twenty-four hours a day, seven days a week to hit the morphine pump and swab out their mouth. Today people go on and off hospice like birth control pills. They try it for a while, if they like it they stay, if they don't like it they get off, only to come back on at a later date.

Today's hospice residents scoot around in their motorized wheelchairs, popping in and out for a cigarette. On the weekend, they sign themselves out to go camping, canoeing, skydiving etc. and sign themselves back in Sunday night.

They even have THE HOSPICE FIVE HUNDRED, where fifty hospice patients hop in their motorized wheel chairs, equipped with pill containers, beer holder and ashtray. For the obese hospice patient, the motorized scooter comes equipped with a pole for the IV of their choice Sweet and Low, Equal, or Splenda, so as to maintain proper hydration.

CHAPTER 24

Goodbye Feudalcare
El Fin

FeudalCare was closed forever by the state (Natzi's) on 1/1/2011. Unbeknownst to President Dee Dee a state inspector (Natzi) popped in that day. As always Nurse Dee had with her the only thing that could possibly love her, her dog Crumpits. Shortly before the inspector (Natzi) arrived, Crumpits took a dump right in the middle of the floor. The inspector (Natzi) did not see it. When he stepped in it, he fell and slid, ruining his three thousand-dollar Armani Suit! Turns out that was the least of his problems though. He broke his elbow when he fell, and then was savagely attacked by the dog! The man remains in traction till this day.

Printed in the United States
by Baker & Taylor Publisher Services